PRAISE FOR *STRANGER THINGS HAVE HAPPENED*

★ "Leave[s] readers weak with laughter."

—*Booklist*, Starred Review

"Strand maintains a taut pace with cliff-hanger endings to each chapter."

—*School Library Journal*

PRAISE FOR *THE GREATEST ZOMBIE MOVIE EVER*

"A funny and spirited romp."

—Kirkus Reviews

"Fans of comical books rejoice as Strand has hit the zombie trend on its head with this one... Aspiring filmmakers, zombie movie fans, and reluctant readers should be entertained by this title."

—School Library Journal

"Readers will come away not only with stomachs aching from laughter but with the stars in their own eyes a little brighter for following Justin's rocky progress."

—Booklist

"[Strand] hits his stride with sarcastic conversation and the relationship dynamics. This novel will appeal to anyone trying to create something great against all odds—or anyone who needs a laugh."

—RT Book Reviews

PRAISE FOR *I HAVE A BAD FEELING ABOUT THIS*

"Fans of Strand's other novels of outrageous circumstance…
will not be disappointed. A delightfully ludicrous read."

—*School Library Journal*

"Just the thing for teen wiseacres who don't mind a bucket or
three of blood."

—*Booklist*

PRAISE FOR *A BAD DAY FOR VOODOO*

"Jeff Strand is the funniest writer in the game, and *A Bad Day for Voodoo* is wicked, wicked fun. Dark, devious, and delicious!"

> —Jonathan Maberry, *New York Times* bestselling
> author of *Rot & Ruin* and *Flesh & Bone*

"Humor and horror collide in Strand's YA debut."

> —*Publishers Weekly*

"For a reader intentionally seeking a wacky horror/comedy, this book delivers."

> —*VOYA*

HOW YOU RUINED MY LIFE

ALSO BY JEFF STRAND

HOW YOU RUINED MY LIFE

JEFF STRAND

sourcebooks
fire

Published by Sourcebooks Fire, an imprint of Sourcebooks, Inc.
P.O. Box 4410, Naperville, Illinois 60567-4410
(630) 961-3900
Fax: (630) 961-2168
sourcebooks.com

Library of Congress Cataloging-in-Publication Data

Names: Strand, Jeff, author.
Title: How you ruined my life / Jeff Strand.
Description: Naperville, Illinois : Sourcebooks Fire, [2018] | Summary: Rod's life is going well until his rich, prankster cousin, Blake, moves in for three months--moving into his room and moving in on his girlfriend and band--ruining everything.
Identifiers: LCCN 2017037472 | (13 : alk. paper)
Subjects: | CYAC: Cousins--Fiction. | Dating (Social customs)--Fiction. | Bands (Music)--Fiction. | Punk rock music--Fiction. | Family life--Fiction.
Classification: LCC PZ7.S8963 How 2018 | DDC [Fic]--dc23 LC record available at https://lccn.loc.gov/2017037472

60934320

Source of Production:
Date of Production:
Run Number: 50115

Printed and bound in the United States of America.
VP 10 9 8 7 6 5 4 3 2 1

This book is dedicated to the kind people who've never actively tried to ruin my life. You know who you are!

1.

THANKS FOR COMING out tonight! Are you ready to *rock*?"

A couple of people in the audience indicate that yes, they are indeed ready to begin the process of rocking. A few others don't look up from their cell phones, but I'm confident that they'll discover their readiness to rock as soon as we start playing. The rest of the eleven or so people in the club haven't bothered to walk over to the dance floor. Presumably, they're waiting for the headline act before committing to whether or not they're mentally and physically prepared to rock.

"We're Fanged Grapefruit," I say into the microphone. "This first song is an original called, 'You Can't Train a Goldfish to Catch Popcorn in Its Mouth, So Don't Even Try.' *One, two, three, go!*"

I can't remember which of us came up with the name Fanged Grapefruit. I think it was Clarissa, our drummer. I consider myself the creative driving force of the band, but if you see Clarissa, you'll understand why she doesn't lose many arguments. She's at least six foot three (though I've never measured her), and you wouldn't want to arm wrestle her unless you were willing to lose an arm. When she really gets going, her drumsticks become a blur. And when she's done with a set, the sticks look like they've been gnawed on by beavers.

Mel, short for Melvin, is lead guitar and background vocals. I'm lead vocals and rhythm guitar. Ironically, Mel is a worse guitar player and a better singer than me. Not everything we do in Fanged Grapefruit makes sense.

Mel doesn't look like he should be in a punk rock band. He looks like he should be president of the Chess Club. Which he is, but I assure you, the guy plays chess with *attitude*. He also gets straight A's and is likely to be our class valedictorian, and if so, I hope he'll pause his inspiring commencement speech for a wicked guitar solo.

I'm Rod, short for Rodney. Nice to meet you. I'm pretty much average, I guess.

Other band names we'd brainstormed included Untidy Reptiles, Autocorrected Text Fail, Rod & the Whacknuts, Carnivorous Vegans, Impolite Music for Unruly People, The RMC Experiment, Say Goodbye to Your Ears, Pawn Takes Rook, Crunchy Noise, Crispy Noise, Chicken Fried Noise,

(The Parentheticals), Apes with Monkey Faces, Hairnets Gloriously Aflame, Dog Eat Dog Eat Munchkin, The Self-Diagnosing Hypochondriacs, Sequel II, and Sushi Gun.

We play at this club, the Lane, every Monday, which is the only day you can get in if you're under eighteen. We go onstage around eight, and we're home by nine fifteen, so all our parents are cool with us being out on a school night. It also helps that they've never actually been inside the Lane, which is a bubbling pit of health code violations. If you have to go to the bathroom, hold it. Trust me.

I'm sure we'd have a much bigger audience if we could play on a Friday or Saturday night, but Clarissa, Mel, and I are only sixteen, so we've got a couple of years to go. (Sorry if it was insulting that I did the math for you.) We hope that by the time we're old enough to play there on a weekend, we'll have upgraded to venues where your feet don't stick to the floor as often.

Anyway, we begin to rock out on our guitars and drums, and select members of the audience begin to move to the music. Well, okay, only two of them. And one is my girlfriend, Audrey. You might say that she doesn't count, but we got together because I was in a band, so I think she *does* count, thank you very much.

Audrey runs our merch table. We never sell anything,

though she gives away free stickers to people who look like they might be band managers. She's as tiny as Clarissa is non-tiny. You won't believe me if I say she's the most gorgeous girl at our school, so all I'll say is that if you look at her and look at me, you'd say, "Wow, how did that happen? He must be in a band."

By the end of our set, three people in the audience are bopping their heads to the music. That's a fifty percent increase from when we started. Fanged Grapefruit rules!

After dropping off Clarissa, Mel, and then Audrey (because I always pick her up first and drop her off last, even though she lives the furthest away), I go home, take a shower, and start packing my lunch for the next day.

"How was your gig?" Mom asks, walking into the kitchen.

"Great! Every show gets a little better."

"I was going to do that for you," she says, pointing to the sandwich I'm making.

"I know." Mom works two jobs, both of which suck, so I'm always happy to make my own lunch. Plus I'm very specific about the spread of my peanut butter. It should be as close to the edge of the bread as possible without spilling over, and the thickness should be consistent. Generally, I'm a pretty casual guy, but not when it comes to peanut butter application. We all have our quirks.

"I've got news," she says.

"Dad got out of prison?"

Dad isn't really in prison. He left us two years ago. We joke about him being in prison as a coping mechanism.

"No."

"I'm finally going to get a baby sister?"

"Ha. You wish."

"You got a raise?"

Mom shakes her head. "I did get a five-dollar tip on an eighteen-dollar meal though. That was nice."

"Wild panthers have run amok in our neighborhood, gobbling up people left and right?"

"Maybe you should stop guessing."

"Maybe I should. So is this good news or bad news?" I ask.

"Well…"

I set down the butter knife. "That doesn't sound like a good 'well…'"

"I wouldn't necessarily call it *bad* news," Mom says. "It's definitely not the worst news ever. Nobody died or anything."

"Tell me."

"You know your aunt Mary and uncle Clark?"

"Of course." I don't think I've seen Uncle Clark since I was six. We live in Florida, and they live in California. He and Dad never got along, so every couple of years, Aunt Mary would visit us by herself. With Dad out of the picture, I assumed we'd see more of our extended family, but it never really happened.

"Aunt Mary and Uncle Clark are going on a cruise."

"That's cool." I consider that for a moment and then get very excited. "Are they taking us with them?"

"No."

"Oh."

"It's one of those around-the-world cruises. Three whole months. Doesn't that sound fun?"

Did I mention that Aunt Mary and Uncle Clark are rich? You probably picked up on that when Mom said they were going on a three-month-long world cruise.

"Is Blake going with them?" I ask.

"No. He's not."

Suddenly, I have an idea where this conversation is headed. It doesn't make me happy. "Maybe you should spell this out for me," I say.

"Your cousin Blake is going to live with us for three months. Isn't that exciting?"

I stare at her for a few hours.

(Possibly, I'm exaggerating.)

"Starting when?" I ask.

"Next week."

"You mean before the school year ends?"

"Yes. He's going to transfer to your school."

"That's messed up!"

Mom shrugs. "They got a good deal on the cruise."

"Where's he going to stay? We don't have a guest bedroom."

"Well, I thought…you know…"

"He can't share my room!" If I wasn't almost an adult, I would have stomped my foot.

"Honey, it's only for three months."

"That's a quarter of a year! I thought we were broke," I say. "How are we going to pay for all that extra food?"

"We're not *that* broke, and obviously, your aunt and uncle will help pay for groceries."

"Isn't he a spoiled brat?"

"You haven't seen him in ten years," Mom says.

"Well, ten years ago he was a spoiled brat."

"I'm sure he's fine now."

"Doesn't he have any friends he can stay with in California?"

My mom sighs. "Rodney, he's family. Family is always welcome in our home."

I hope I'm not coming off as whiny and selfish. If a hurricane tore the roof off their house and they lost all of their worldly possessions, sure, I'd happily donate half of my room to Cousin Blake while they rebuilt their lives. But asking me to give up my privacy so Aunt Mary and Uncle Clark can go on a luxury cruise seems kind of unreasonable.

However, I'm pretty sure this is a done deal, and my mom has enough stress in her life without me continuing to protest.

"All right," I say.

"Thank you." Mom gives me a hug. "I think you'll enjoy having him here."

Who knows? Maybe I will. Maybe my cousin is a really cool guy. Maybe he has good taste in music. And maybe he's witty and entertaining. And maybe he'll be willing to help with emergency cleanup if we're having a wild party and Mom calls suddenly to say she's on her way home early.

We might end up being the best friends that any two cousins could ever be. We'll giggle and frolic and be inseparable.

But probably not.

I can't believe I have to share my room.

I return to making my lunch. I'll try to be optimistic and pretend that these will be the best three months of my life. How bad could it be?

2.

UPON FIRST GLANCE into my bedroom, you can be forgiven for believing that I'm a vile, disgusting slob. Organization of my personal belongings is not one of my strongest traits.

But it's not like there are dirty dishes or long-forgotten pizzas or sweaty clothes that have been on the floor for more than forty-eight hours. If you see anything that's green, it was always that color. Gas masks, though a nice fashion accessory, are completely unnecessary to breathe the air. Your pets would be perfectly safe in there.

C'mon, I'm in a punk rock band! You wouldn't want my room to be immaculate, would you? Nah. My current housekeeping, where it takes a moment to figure out which mound is the desk and which is the bed, is the way to go. And though it may look messy to an outsider, there's sort of a method to the madness. I can usually find stuff I'm looking for on the seventh or eighth try.

I like my room the way it is, but I have this sneaking suspicion that Mom will ask me to clean it before Blake arrives. I can't blame her for that. Blake might be a raging neat freak, and I don't want to start off on a bad note.

I stand in the doorway for a moment, surveying my room and trying to work out a plan of cleaning attack. If I had a bulldozer, I could just push everything from one half of the room to the other and be done with it. Sadly, I don't own a bulldozer, and the hallway to my bedroom is too narrow to get one through. We have a one-story house, so technically, I could drive a bulldozer through the wall, but that would end up making more of a mess, don't you think?

Yes, I am procrastinating on cleaning my room by thinking about driving a bulldozer through the side of my house. Welcome to my mind.

Actually, while I'm procrastinating, let me take you on a quick tour of my house. Let's start from the outside. Yep, it's the small, light blue one. The car that doesn't look like it would start is mine. We're in an okay neighborhood, I guess. Nobody has swimming pools, but they also don't have zombies chained in their backyard.

Wipe your feet on the "Welcome Friends" mat and come on in. (Fun fact: that doormat is older than I am.) Congratulations! You're in my living room! That's one ugly couch, huh? It's more comfortable than it looks. Don't bother checking the cushions for loose change. I've got that covered.

From the couch you can see the kitchen, which is where I was making the peanut butter sandwich I talked about earlier. On the refrigerator door, there's a flier that I made for the first-ever performance of Fanged Grapefruit. Mom hung it there like an elementary school art project. I don't mean to brag, but if you open the refrigerator, there may be some food inside.

There's the hallway that's too narrow for a bulldozer. First door on the left leads to the bathroom. You'll be pleased to know that it's equipped with all the modern conveniences—a toilet, a sink with hot and cold running water, and a shower. Plus a fully stocked library.

The second and last door on the left leads to Mom's room. Nothing to see there. The first and only door on the right leads to my room, which we've already discussed. (Recap: it's very untidy.)

And…well, I guess that's it, except for the garage. But you can't look in there because it's where we keep our newly restored Ferrari. Oh, yeah. It's worth a fortune. The windows are made of diamonds. No, no, don't open the door. I wouldn't make that up. Just trust me.

All right, time to clean my room.

Did I do a perfect job? No.

Can you see most of the floor now? Yes.

I took a "before" picture so that if Blake has a problem with it, I can prove that I made an effort.

I didn't tell you, but I called Audrey before I started and asked if she wanted to help clean. Her response was, and I quote, "Ha ha. No."

If I were a good son, I'd clean up the rest of the house.

And you know what? I'm a good son.

I don't get down and scrub the corners or anything, but I do a perfectly adequate job. It's not like an emperor or Jennifer Lawrence is coming to visit.

When I'm finished, I survey my work, proud of a job well done. When Mom gets home, she thanks me and expresses surprise that I cleaned the house so soon since Cousin Blake won't be here for six more days.

Five days later, the house looks the way it did before I started cleaning.

Oh well. I'll clean it again after band practice.

Mel and Clarissa are in my garage, which has no Ferrari, blasting our song "Jalapeño Poppers Filled with Battery Acid Are a Tasty Treat." (We have long song titles.)

This song requires a lot of screeching on my part, which hurts my voice after a while, so we take a quick break for me to drink some water with lemon and honey.

"When does your cousin get here?" Mel asks.

"Tomorrow."

"That's crazy, dude. I wouldn't give up half my room."

"It's not like I have a choice."

"Make him sleep out in a tent."

"It'll be fine."

"You'll have a roommate when you go to college," says Clarissa. "Might as well get used to it."

"He's not going to ask to be part of the band, is he?" asks Mel. "Because we're a well-oiled machine, and we can't go messing up the dynamic."

"One, he's not going to ask to join the band," I say. "Two, we're not a well-oiled machine. We're a decently oiled machine. And the way I look at it, my cousin Blake moving in means one extra friendly face in the crowd every week."

"He'd better not cramp our style. We've worked hard on it," Mel grumbles.

"If he cramps our style, I will personally make sure he's removed from the premises."

"Are you sure he's not going to say, 'Hey, I play the harp. Can I be in the band?'"

"A harp might be an interesting addition to our sound," says Clarissa.

"Stop worrying about him," I tell Mel. "If anything, it sounds like he'll want to join Chess Club."

"Oh, he can't join Chess Club. We've got the perfect blend of skill levels and personalities. If he joins, he'll throw off the whole balance."

"You're not a very welcoming person," says Clarissa.

"I've never claimed to be. That's why Rod is the one who welcomes our audience to the show."

"It'll be fine," I say.

"What if he steals from you?"

"I'll know it was him."

"What if he steals stuff you won't miss until he's gone?"

"If I don't notice it's gone for three months, I don't need it."

"What if he robs you blind on the last day?" Mel asks.

"You seem very upset about this," says Clarissa. "Do you need a hug?"

"I'm just watching out for Rod."

"I'm not gonna lie," I say. "When my mom first told me the news, I was kind of annoyed. But really, what's the big deal? So my cousin's staying with us for a while. So what? I barely know anything about him. Of all the bad things that could happen to me, this is pretty low on the list."

"I suppose it's not as bad as getting buried alive," says Mel.

"Nope."

"And it's not as bad as, like, getting punched in the stomach when you weren't expecting it and you'd just had spicy food."

"Nope."

"And it's not as bad as the sun exploding. That would cause problems for everyone."

"Anyway," I say before he can come up with a fourth example, "it's not ideal, but I've come to terms with it. So let's just worry about making the world *rock*!"

We resume playing. I like to think that we're rocking so hard that the house is coming apart, but the cracks in the wall were already there.

Nine songs later (our songs are short), Clarissa stops playing. "Is that your doorbell?"

We stop to listen. The doorbell rings again, so I press the button to open the garage door.

There's a U-Haul truck parked in our driveway and a man standing at our front door. He walks over to the garage and smiles. "Hi," he says, "I'm looking for Louise Conklin."

"She's at work. I'm her son."

"Okay, I'm the mover. I've got stuff here from Blake Montgomery."

"Excuse me?" I ask.

The man points to the truck. "I'm delivering boxes from California."

"Oh. Uh, okay."

I follow him to the back of the truck. The man slides open the door, revealing that it's completely filled with cardboard boxes.

"How many of those are his?" I ask.

"All of 'em."

"Are you kidding me?"

"Yeah, I drove all the way from California to Florida to play a little joke. Got nothing better to do with my time. I hope it was funny enough."

"You're being sarcastic now, right?"

"Yeah."

"Okay, well, huh. I guess just put the boxes in the garage for now. We'll move our stuff out of the way."

The man shakes his head. "I only drive. I don't unload."

Mel, Clarissa, and I unload forty-two boxes from the back of the truck and stack them in the garage. Only three of them are light boxes. For a few, Mel and I have to say, "Um, Clarissa, could you get this one?" Several require teamwork.

When we're finally done, the man stands there expectantly.

"What?" I ask.

"Tip?"

"Nah."

He gets back in the U-Haul and drives away.

"What do you think are in these?" asks Mel.

"Bricks," I say.

"Are you sure he's not moving in permanently?"

"I'm not sure of anything anymore."

"Did you know he was sending all this?" asks Clarissa.

"Nope," I say. "I sure didn't."

"Seems like a lot of stuff for three months," Mel adds.

"It certainly does."

We all stand there for a moment.

"Well," says Mel, "I'm sure there's a logical explanation for all this stuff, besides him planning to completely take over your home. Is it safe to say that practice is over now that there's no room for us in your garage?"

"Yeah, we're done for today. Blake must not know that we

have a small house. He'll have to put most of this in a storage unit. He'll be here tomorrow, so we'll figure it out then."

"Good luck to you, dude."

"Thanks." And I mean it.

"Hey, Mom," I say when she walks in the front door. "Come over here. I want to show you something."

I take her into the garage.

"Where did all this come from?" she asks.

"Blake sent them across the country in a U-Haul."

"All of them?" She looks a bit bewildered.

"Yep. Especially the really heavy ones."

Mom frowns. "That seems like something we should have discussed beforehand."

"You'd think so."

"Is this everything he owns?"

"I don't know what he owns."

"I'll talk to Aunt Mary."

"Kinda late," I say. "Blake's stuff is already here."

"You're right. You're right. Sorry about this, Rod."

"Is my cousin a weirdo?"

"No, he's not a weirdo."

"Don't get me wrong. I love weirdos. I'm a proud weirdo. Normal people are boring. But there's good weird, and there's bad weird. And sending forty-two heavy boxes of stuff without telling us first feels like Blake might be the bad kind."

"We'll get this sorted out," Mom assures me. "The next three months are going to be fun, I promise."

I'm not sure I believe her.

3.

MOM HAS TO work, so I volunteered to pick Blake up at the airport. If I hadn't volunteered, she would have asked me to do it, but by preemptively making the offer, I get credit for volunteering to do something I would've had to do anyway. It's all about the timing.

I drive into the Arrivals area, which is filled with airport employees blowing whistles (Whistles are fun!) but doing little to actually direct traffic. I see Blake sitting on a bench at the end of the row. He doesn't look much different than when he was a little kid. He's still short, a bit chubby, and he has perfectly combed blond hair. His face is extremely red.

Blake isn't carrying any luggage, which is a relief.

However, there's a porter standing next to him with a baggage cart that has, I'd estimate, a dozen suitcases. Good thing those don't belong to Blake. That would be ridiculous. Absurd *and* ridiculous. Just plain wacky.

I pull up to the curb beside him, put the car in park, and get out. "Hi, Blake!" I say, waving.

Blake regards me the way you'd look at somebody who has long, wet boogers dangling from each nostril that are flapping in the wind. I do a quick nose check to make sure that's not the case. My nostrils are clear.

"Hello, Rodney," he says. "Is that your car?"

It seems like an odd question, since he literally just saw me drive up in this particular automobile. It's like he's offering me the opportunity to say, "Oh, goodness gracious no. I don't drive this old thing! My real car is currently having the stereo system upgraded, so I was forced to borrow this one from the junkyard at the last minute."

"Yep, it's all mine," I say.

Blake frowns. "Hmm."

Hey, I'm proud to own a car! I don't have to listen to Blake hmm-ing mine. "Do you have any luggage?" I ask.

Blake gestures to the porter.

"All of that?"

Blake nods. "It's for three long months."

"I know, but… I… A lot of boxes showed up at…" I decide that this conversation can wait. "I'm not sure we can fit all of that in my car."

"I'm sure we can't," says Blake. "That's why I assumed you'd bring a more appropriate vehicle."

"We can make it work," I counter. If we fill the trunk, the

back seat, make Blake sit on a couple of suitcases, and strap the rest to the roof, we *might* be able to fit everything, though my car probably won't move.

"We can store some of the luggage for you," says the porter. "You could make a second trip."

Blake sighs. "I've never been fond of second trips."

"It'll be fine," I say. "I don't live that far from here."

"I suppose I could hire another car and driver," says Blake.

"It's really not necessary," I insist. I open the trunk, pull the first suitcase off the cart, and slide it in the back. As I pick up the second suitcase, I notice that Blake remains seated on the bench.

He's not going to sit there and *watch* me load his luggage, is he?

Apparently, he is.

I'm not sure if I should say something or go ahead and load up the car. I decide that since we've got a quarter of a year together, it's best not to get off to a tense start.

I'm able to fit about half of his suitcases into my car. "Okay," I say since Blake has yet to stand. "I think we're ready to go."

Blake sighs again.

He still hasn't gotten up. Does he think I'm going to carry him to the car? Nobody could be *that* lazy, right?

I suddenly wonder if Blake uses a wheelchair to get around. Am I the most horrible person in the world for thinking he was lazy? Am I a monster?

No. Of course not. My mom would've said something before I picked him up at the airport. And there's no wheelchair nearby.

Finally, Blake stands, moving as if a dozen steel rhinoceroses are strapped to his back. He slowly waddles over to my car and gets in the front seat, grunting with the effort.

I close the trunk and get in the car. Blake hasn't shut his door.

"Your door's still open," I tell him, trying to be helpful.

"I'm aware."

"I thought you might consider closing it so we can go."

"Hmm."

Is he testing me? Maybe he's trying to figure out if, during these crucial first minutes of our relationship, he can make me his personal servant. Or he may be messing with me. I can't tell. Either way, even though I don't want to pick a fight with the guy, I have to assert myself.

"Look," I say, "my job is to welcome you and make you feel at home. I'm happy to do it. But this isn't the kind of deal where I open and close car doors for you like a limo driver."

"I definitely didn't mistake this for a limo."

"It's a perfectly good car," I insist.

Blake runs his index finger along the dashboard. "Could be cleaner."

"Close the door, Blake."

The porter walks over and closes the door for him. Blake gives me a smug grin.

I glare at him. "Do you need somebody to fasten your seat belt for you?"

Blake puts on his own seat belt. One of the airport employees angrily blows his whistle at me, and I drive us out of the Arrivals area.

"So how was your flight?" I ask.

Blake shrugs. "It was an airplane ride. You know it didn't crash because I'm here with you now, so what else is there to say about it?"

I have the sudden realization that my cousin Blake may, in fact, be a jerk.

"Well," I say, "you could have been sitting behind a shrieking baby. Or you could have sat next to Tom Hanks. Those are the kind of details you could have shared."

"Why would Tom Hanks be on my flight?"

"Why wouldn't he be? You don't think Tom Hanks has millions of frequent flier miles?"

"I suppose."

"All I'm saying is that there are plenty of interesting things that could happen when you're flying that don't involve fiery deaths."

"I'm not a fan of meaningless small talk," Blake informs me. "How was your drive to the airport? See? That was annoying, wasn't it?"

"My drive over was fine. No traffic problems."

"I didn't care about your answer, and you didn't care about sharing it with me."

"Are you saying that we shouldn't talk for three months?"

Blake shakes his head. "I believe people should talk about important things."

"I'm all for that. But as human beings in, y'know, society, there are ways that we communicate. I'm not going to pick you up after not having seen you for years and immediately ask, 'So, Blake, do you believe in life after death?'"

"I'd prefer that."

"No, you wouldn't. You'd be weirded out."

"Very well."

Very well? Nobody says "very well" in the real world, do they? I wonder how much trouble I'd get in if I drove over to Departures and shoved him out the door.

"Are you messing with me?" I ask.

"Why would you think that?"

"Because you're acting like somebody who's messing with somebody. People don't actually behave like that. I'm not sure if you know this, but your behavior is really, really abnormal. As in, you are literally the strangest person I've ever encountered, and I'm in a punk rock band."

"You're in a band?"

"Yeah."

Blake nods his approval. "That's cool."

"Thanks."

"Sorry," says Blake. "I don't interact with people much."

"I can see that."

"I get nervous when I meet new people, even though you're not technically a new person, and I don't present the best version of myself. I can be kind of odd."

"Yeah, I picked up on that." Okay, I decide that if Blake is willing to admit his oddness, I should forgive him and move on. "It's okay. I'm not the most socially amazing person either."

"Your car is fine."

"Thank you."

"It smells nice."

"It shouldn't smell like anything."

"Maybe it's your deodorant."

"Let's switch topics," I suggest.

"Sorry. Was that creepy?"

"It was getting there."

"Sometimes my oddness crosses over into creepiness."

"It's fine," I insist.

"I'm not usually the kind of person who compliments deodorant. Just so you know."

"Here's what we're going to try," I say. "We're not going to talk for the rest of the drive to my house. I'll put on some music, and we'll listen to it. That'll give us time to recalibrate our brains and make sure they're in good working order before we start talking again. Sound okay?"

Blake nods.

I turn on the stereo. One of my favorite bands, Infamously Vicious, blasts the song "Rabid to the Core."

Blake scowls. Two seconds in and I can tell he isn't enjoying this song.

"That's not your band, is it?" he asks.

"No."

"Good."

"They're not trying for mass appeal," I explain.

"Clearly."

"It's not important to be liked by everybody," I say. "The worst thing in the world is to be mediocre."

"I completely agree," says Blake. "But if there's a line in

the air that says, 'mediocre,' it's probably better to be above it than below it."

I turn off the music.

"You didn't have to turn it off," says Blake. "It was bad, but it wasn't literally hurting me."

"We're going to try silence," I say. "No music, no talking, simply the sound of the wind."

"You mean the sound of your engine."

"Whatever."

"You should get it checked out."

"I will."

"Automobiles aren't supposed to sound like this."

"My car is fine."

"I actually felt safer with the music playing," says Blake. "There's a lot of stuff going on with this car. I assume the only reason your 'check engine' light isn't on is because it's burnt out."

"I thought we were going to try silence."

"I thought we were too, but your car had other ideas."

I turn the stereo back on and eject the CD. "Fine. You pick a radio station."

Blake goes through the entire FM dial and then through the entire AM dial and then through most of the FM dial again before choosing something Auto-Tuned and horrible.

It's only three months, I tell myself. *Only three months. Only three long, endless, excruciating months.*

4.

WE PULL INTO my driveway. For the first time ever, I'm kind of embarrassed by the size of my house. I wish we had a heliport on the roof or something.

I turn off the engine. I'd never noticed it before, but my car takes a while to wind down after it's shut off. It whirrs and sputters and sounds like it's desperately trying to cling to precious life, as if it knows in its heart that it may never turn on again.

"Well, we both survived," says Blake, unfastening his seat belt. "I assumed we would, but there were moments of doubt."

"Yep," I say in a lighthearted tone, pretending that I think he's kidding around. I unfasten my own seat belt and get out of the car.

Blake has not yet opened his door.

I really hope we're not doing the whole door thing again. If Blake thinks I'm going to open his door for him, he's whack-a-doodle nuts. That is *not* the dynamic we're going to establish here. I will leave him in the car all night before I open that door for him.

"C'mon," I say, gesturing to my house and hoping it sends the message, *Hey, it's time for you to open the car door—all by yourself—and exit the vehicle.*

Blake looks at me expectantly.

Maybe I'll just open the door a bit and let him push it the rest of the...

No! No, no, no, no! I will not open the door for him. He may be used to that kind of treatment back in Rich McWealthy Goldcash Treasure Land, but he's our houseguest now. We're not on a date. In my world, you open your own door. No porter is going to save him this time.

I go to the back of the car and open the trunk. I grab a couple of suitcases and then walk past the passenger side, hoping he'll notice what's happening and decide to become a participant.

He's still sitting there.

If he were busy checking his phone or something, *maybe* I'd be okay with it. But as far as I can tell, my able-bodied cousin is, indeed, waiting for me to open his door like a chauffeur. Nope. Not gonna happen.

Maybe he'll give me a tip.

Even then, nope. Nope, nope, nope, nopeity nope. If you don't have a broken arm, I'm not going to be his door opener. Nope.

I walk up to my house, set down his suitcases, and unlock the front door. I do this slowly, waiting to hear the sound of the car door opening.

I do not hear this sound.

Could he be too dumb to figure out how to work a door handle? I'd happily take a dullard of a cousin over one who thinks I'm his butler.

I open the front door, hoping he'll see how easy and fun it is and decide to follow my lead. I take his suitcases inside, carry them down the hallway, and put them in my bedroom.

When I walk back outside, Blake is still sitting in the car, staring at me.

What I'd like to do is roll down the window, shove a fire hose in there, and fill the car with water until Blake takes the hint. If I had a box of scorpions, I'd toss them inside as incentive. Unfortunately, I don't even have one scorpion, much less a whole box. (Lesson: plan ahead.)

I'd call my mom, but that would be tattling. Sixteen-year-old lead vocalists in punk rock bands aren't tattletales. Instead I try to reason with my cousin.

I casually stroll over to the car. "Everything okay?"

I ask, speaking loudly enough to be heard through the window.

"Everything's fine."

"Would you like a tour of the house?"

"Seems kind of small to require an actual tour."

"Would you like a tour of my fist?"

Whoa. I can't believe I said that. I haven't offered to punch somebody since I was in third grade and this kid Cody dropped a goldfish down the back of my shirt. (The goldfish was traumatized but survived.) I wouldn't really hit Blake, of course, but maybe it wouldn't be so bad if he believes I'm a scary, short-fused stick of TNT-level rage.

Blake narrows his eyes. "Are you threatening me?"

"Nah."

"That sounded like a threat."

It suddenly occurs to me that a rich kid like Blake could have a squad of goons at his disposal. I don't want to wake up in the middle of night to frightening men in face masks standing next to my bed, wielding baseball bats.

No, that's silly. Still, Mom will be pretty upset if I invited our new houseguest to examine my knuckles at a high velocity.

"It was a joke," I say. "But you can't keep insulting my car and house."

"You're confusing insults with observations. If I make an

observation and you take it as an insult, maybe it's time to reevaluate your life."

I sure hope that you're on my side as you're reading this. I believe I've presented a fair and accurate depiction of the events thus far. So what do you think? Am I wrong for wanting to drag Blake out of my car through the windshield? He's the worst person ever, right?

Don't answer that literally. Obviously, there are worse people (Hitler, Stalin, Freddy Krueger, etc.), but he's terrible!

How would you handle this? Politely? Impolitely? Would you start tearing out your hair? Would you shout "Gaaaahhhhhhh!!!" at the top of your lungs for several minutes? I could really use some guidance.

I settle for giving Blake a dirty look. Then I grab a couple more suitcases, muttering words under my breath that will get the publisher of this book in trouble if I share them here. As I walk past the car, I say, "I'll meet you inside. Come on in when you're ready."

Inside my house, I drop his suitcases in my bedroom and then sit down on the living room couch.

I can't believe I'm sixteen years old and spending my Saturday afternoon engaged in a battle of wills with my cousin. What's his deal? Did Aunt Mary and Uncle Clark raise him to be like this, or was there a chemical spill in the hospital where he was born? Was he kicked in the head by a mule? Is he pure evil?

I turn on the television. Some guy with a yappy voice is demonstrating how astonishing a pasta maker can be. The studio audience oohs and aahs in amazement. There's a close-up of a woman who seems to be almost in tears over how much this pasta maker will change her life. I switch channels.

I stop at *Gerbils v. Otters*, an animated show that has gotten amazing mileage out of the concept of gerbils fighting otters. I haven't seen this episode before, so it's a good way to pass the time until my ridiculous cousin joins me.

The episode ends, and another begins.

Then that episode ends, and another begins.

Then *that* episode ends, and another begins.

I want to check on Blake, but I don't want him to see me peeking through the curtains. Instead I go into the kitchen and make myself a sandwich.

Isn't Blake hungry? Doesn't he have to go to the bathroom?

He'd better not be using my automobile as a restroom.

Mom will be home from work in a couple of hours. I hope this power struggle is over by then. It will be a difficult situation to explain.

I enjoy my delicious sandwich and a small bag of potato chips while I watch another episode. My weekends are not typically spent sitting on the couch and watching TV, but these are extreme circumstances.

I wonder what Blake would do if I waved my sandwich in front of the window.

(I don't wave my sandwich in front of the window.)

I'd like to end this war, but if I don't stand up for myself, it's going to be an unbearable three months. I mean, it's clearly going to be an unbearable three months anyway, but it'll be even worse if I don't put my foot down.

My phone vibrates. It's a text message from Audrey: How's it going with your cousin?

He won't come out of the car, I text back.

??????, Audrey responds.

I'm serious. He expects me to open the door for him.

???????????, Audrey texts since there is no emoji strong enough to convey her bewilderment.

Incoming call from Audrey. Yep, things are so crazy that we're going to talk instead of text. I tap Accept.

"What do you mean he expects you to open the door for him?" she demands.

"He seriously thinks I should be his chauffeur. The guy is messed up."

"How long has he been sitting out there?"

"Three and a half episodes of *Gerbils v. Otters*."

"*What?*"

"I know, right? Dude's peculiar."

"Shouldn't you just let him out of the car?" asked Audrey. "What if he suffocates?"

"He's not going to suffocate," I say, although I'm suddenly not so sure. Based on the very limited amount of time I've spent with him, Cousin Blake may very well be the kind of person who would let himself run out of air simply to teach me a valuable lesson.

I get off the couch and hurry over to the front window. I'm sure there's plenty of oxygen left in the car, but what if he's breathing really deeply to purposely use it up?

There's a knock at the door.

I'm almost positive it's not our next-door neighbor here to inform me there's blue kid in my car, but I have a split second of panic anyway.

"I've gotta go," I tell Audrey. I disconnect the call and put the phone in my pocket. Then I open the door.

It is, of course, Blake. His face is redder than usual.

"Where's your bathroom?" he asks.

I point to the hallway. "First door on the left."

Blake hurries down the hall. I don't feel a huge sense of accomplishment since all I did was outwait his bladder, but still, I won this round.

I'm not sure what I'll do if he goes back to the car after he's done. Probably let out a primal scream or something.

I decide that it can't hurt to get a couple more of his suitcases. As I bring them inside, Blake steps out of the bathroom, looking sheepish.

"Nature called," he explains.

"I figured."

He takes a deep breath as if composing himself. "I can't help but feel that it's possible we may have gotten off to a bad start."

"Yeah."

"Sorry."

"You apologized before. A better technique would be to change your behavior."

"I didn't apologize before."

"Yes, you did."

"That doesn't sound like me," Blake says.

"Maybe it wasn't a sincere, heartfelt apology, but you said sorry a couple of times."

"Oh," says Blake. "I don't remember that. Anyway, I understand why you think you're too good to open the door for me. We all want to rise above our station. If you'd rather I open my own doors from now on, I'll respect that decision."

"Yes, I'd rather you do that," I say. "I really, really would."

"It's a deal then," says Blake, extending his hand.

It seems weird that I should have to shake his hand to make an agreement that I'm not his servant, but I decide that if he's (once again) willing to make an effort, I won't protest. I shake his hand, which is cold and clammy like his soul.

"What are you watching?" he asks.

"*Gerbils v. Otters.*"

"A cartoon?"

"Yeah."

"Hmm."

"What?"

"I don't know many sixteen-year-olds who still watch cartoons."

"What are you talking about? Everybody under fifty watches cartoons," I insist.

"I haven't watched a cartoon since I was seven," says Blake.

"What an empty life you must have lived."

"All I'm saying is that one of us exists in the real world and the other doesn't."

I shake my head. "Whatever world you think you exist in, it's not the real world."

"Very well. Don't let me stop you from enjoying *Gophers v. Dolphins.*"

"*Gerbils v. Otters.*"

Blake glances around. "So do I get the tour? Oh, wait. I conducted it myself by turning my head."

In a small way, I have to admire his fearlessness. I'm not a muscular guy who juggles barbells, but in a one-on-one weaponless battle, me against Blake, I'd win for sure.

Maybe Blake has weapons.

Nah. I think he's just nuts.

Blake stretches his arms above his head and yawns. "It was a long flight," he says. "I'm going to take a nap."

He walks into my bedroom and closes the door.

There's still plenty of luggage to carry in plus a whole extra trip back to the airport. I was victorious in the waiting game, but I guess Blake wins this round.

5.

I'M TYPICALLY NOT a twitchy person, but I twitch a lot as I carry in the rest of his suitcases and set them in the living room. I can hear Blake snoring through the bedroom door.

Of course he snores. How could it be otherwise?

As I drive back to the airport, I call Audrey and update her on how horrible Blake is. Then I call Mel and tell him how horrible Blake is. Then I call Clarissa and tell her how horrible Blake is. I feel a little better after being able to vent my frustration three times in a row. At least now I don't want to bash other cars off the highway.

I pick up the rest of Blake's luggage. I tip the porter, but I assure you I'll be seeking reimbursement when I get home.

On the way back to my house, I call Audrey, Mel, and Clarissa again just to remind them that I can't stand my cousin.

It's hard to imagine that he and I are related. If our life situations were swapped, would I behave like that? The thought chills me to the bone. I don't think Aunt Mary and Uncle

Clark even wanted to go on the cruise. They probably needed three months away from their son to regain their sanity.

When I get home, I pause at the front door.

No way.

I can't be hearing his snoring from *outside* the house, can I?

Yep. I sure can.

I open the door. The floors are not actually vibrating, but the noise level coming from my bedroom exceeds anything I thought was physically possible. It's like he's in there playing a tuba.

I carry in the rest of his luggage, hoping there's a CPAP machine in one of these suitcases.

You know what? Maybe Blake isn't evil. Maybe he was just tired. He had to get up early for a long flight, and his exhaustion could have manifested itself into the reprehensible creature lurking in my bedroom. I'll bet that when he wakes up from his nap, he'll be a delight.

Four hours later he's still snoring away.

Mom looks a bit surprised as she walks inside. "Goodness."

"Impressive noise level, isn't it?" I ask.

"How long has he been out?"

"A while."

"How are you two getting along?"

"It's like we're brothers instead of cousins."

"Well, that's good."

The snoring stops.

Mom glances at the large pile of suitcases. "Not a light packer, is he?"

"Nope."

"Does he know we already have a garage full of his boxes?"

"I'm pretty sure he does."

My bedroom door opens with a creak. I hadn't ever noticed the sound, but now that I'm hyperaware of the flaws in my home, it definitely creaks. I'll have to douse it with WD-40 before Blake can comment on it.

Blake steps into the hallway. His hair is perfect, and his face is much less red. He looks like he had a very relaxing nap. His face lights up as he sees Mom.

"Aunt Connie!" he says with a smile. "What a pleasure to see you after all these years!" He walks over and gives her a tight hug.

"Great to see you!" says Mom.

"I apologize for not being awake when you got home. It was a long trip, and I didn't sleep well last night. Too excited, I guess."

"Oh, no, that's totally fine," says Mom. "How was your flight?"

"Well, the first leg I had a window seat, which isn't my top choice, but it's better than a middle seat, right?"

"Definitely," says Mom. "There's nothing worse than a middle seat on a plane."

"Fortunately, in the second leg, I had an aisle seat, and that was the longer of the two flights, so it all worked out. And again, I had no real complaints about the window seat. It's just not my favorite of the options."

"I'm a window seat person myself," says Mom.

"I understand the allure," says Blake, nodding. "The aisle seat has more freedom of movement. But the window seat obviously gives you a better view, and it's easier to sleep. You don't have to worry about getting your elbows bumped by the service cart. It's all about personal preference. There's no right or wrong answer. Unless you prefer the middle seat. Anybody who prefers the middle seat is out of their mind."

Blake laughs. Mom laughs. I stare.

"But yeah, it was a perfectly good flight," says Blake. "The woman next to me was a chatterbox, but she was going to see her grandchildren for the first time in three years, so can you blame her? I'm sure I did more than my share of talking when I told my friends about visiting you and Rod. They didn't say anything, but I'd be willing to bet that a few of my buddies were thinking, *We get it! You're excited! Keep it to yourself!*"

Blake and Mom laugh again.

"I'm glad you're settling in," says Mom.

"Oh, yes. Rodney was a great help with my luggage. Clearly, he's had excellent parenting."

Mom smiles. "Thank you. You're so polite."

Blake shrugs. "I guess I've had excellent parenting too."

"Well, make yourself at home. Help yourself to anything in the refrigerator. Tomorrow we'll go grocery shopping to make sure we've got food that you like."

"Thanks, Aunt Connie. I really appreciate it. You must be tired from a hard day at work, so why don't we order a pizza for dinner? Extra cheese. My treat."

"That sounds great," says Mom. She looks at me. "What do you think, Rod?"

I'm still kind of stunned by Blake's act, and I don't like the idea that he's scoring points with my mother. On the other hand, I love pizza. "Sounds good to me."

"Perfect," says Blake. "You two relax, and I'll order it."

Mom goes to her bedroom to change out of her waitress attire. I sit down on the couch, watching as Blake takes out his cell phone.

What game is this guy playing?

Which is the *real* Cousin Blake? The condescending cretin or the shameless suck-up? Is he good at pretending to be evil or evil pretending to be good?

I'm pretty sure that the Blake I picked up from the airport is his true self and that the Blake who spoke to Mom is a fake, alien version of a teenager created to annoy me. I wouldn't be surprised if Blake looked up at me and winked.

Blake looks up at me. He doesn't wink.

"What do you like on your pizza?" he asks.

"Pepperoni."

I expect him to make a comment about how only hillbillies put pepperoni on their pizza, but he simply taps at his cell phone screen. "Anything else?"

"Sausage."

He taps again. "Anything else?"

"Honesty."

"You want honesty on your pizza?"

"What's your deal, Blake?"

"I'm trying to order a pizza. I don't think I could in good conscience let Aunt Connie make us dinner after she's worked so hard all day."

"You know what I mean."

Blake looks up from his phone. "Do I?"

"Don't play dumb with me."

"I've no idea what you're talking about. All I want to do is order a delicious, piping hot pizza for you and your mother. I didn't realize that was so terrible. Am I invading your territory? Are you the one who usually orders the pizza? I apologize if I overstepped my boundaries."

"This has nothing to do with the pizza."

"Was it the fib?"

"Depends which fib you mean."

"I actually had a middle seat on the plane. It was really uncomfortable. It left me tired and cranky and, as we've previously discussed, socially awkward. But I'm better now."

"Uh-huh."

"Rodney, if you don't like pizza, just say so. I'll order you something else. A bowl of grits?"

I stare directly into his eyes. I don't go so far as to point at my eyes with my index and middle finger and then point at him to convey "I'm watching you" in a sinister manner, but I hope he gets the message.

"Pizza's fine," I say.

"Excellent." Blake looks back at his phone. "Pepperoni, sausage…and anything else?"

"Everything. If you're paying for it, put everything on the pizza."

"Anchovies?"

"Everything but anchovies. Actually, double everything. Triple cheese. Make it so they can't close the box."

"I don't think it'll cook properly."

"Pepperoni, sausage, and double cheese is fine," I say. I don't want to sabotage this pizza just to make him pay more.

I'm not sure who wins this round. We'll call it a draw.

6.

BLAKE'S PART OF the pizza is topped with pineapples.

Now, in the heated "pineapples on pizza" debate, I take the controversial stance that pineapples are a perfectly decent pizza topping. Some people scream, "*Unacceptable!*" but I'm not one of them. Pineapple on pizza is fine. No problem there.

If your part of the pizza is *only* pineapple...well, that's weird, right?

I don't mean to offend you if that's the way you choose to eat your pizza. I'm certainly okay with the concept of a veggie pizza, where pineapple chunks coexist with green peppers, mushrooms, etc. But when pineapple is your only ingredient except for cheese, I'm sorry, but I have to shake my head in judgment. I'm not saying that it makes him a bad person. I'm saying that on top of all the other stuff he's done today, it's one extra blotch on his record.

Blake is frustratingly charming while we eat. He's witty and eloquent. He doesn't make gross sounds when he chews, and I'm sure that Mom thinks he's an absolute treat. I keep waiting for him to make a mistake, to give away his true appalling nature, but he never drops the ruse.

After the pizza is gone and he's thrown away the napkins and paper plates, Blake yawns. "Goodness," he says. "You'd think that the nap would've done the trick, but I'm still sleepy."

"You've had a long day," says Mom.

"Yeah, it was exhausting to carry all that luggage," I add.

Mom glares at me. She thinks I'm making a snide comment about the quantity of luggage he brought when I was actually making a much worse comment about the fact that he made me carry it all.

"Very exhausting," says Blake, not giving away that he didn't participate in any of the luggage transport. He yawns again. "I'll see you in the morning. I bet tomorrow will be an even greater pleasure than today, if such a thing is possible."

"Good night," says Mom. "We're glad you're here."

"Good night," I say, not adding anything about being glad that he's here.

Blake walks back to my bedroom and closes the door.

"He's very well-mannered," says Mom.

"Yeah."

"And you were worried that you two might not get along. Sometimes you just have to give people a chance."

"You're right," I say. This is not the time to blab about Blake's dual nature. I'm not saying that I've got a code of honor where I won't squeal. Believe me, if Blake keeps up his behavior, I'll squeal like a mobster ratting out his associates in exchange for immunity and a new identity under the Federal Witness Protection Program even if it means a lifetime of always looking over my shoulder and waiting for the ghosts of my past to make a reappearance. (Sorry if that was melodramatic. It's been a rough day.)

For now, I'll remain optimistic and trust that I can work things out with my cousin. If he knows I'm on to him, he'll have to change his ways. He can't maintain the illusion of not being despicable for three full months.

Mom yawns. "I think I'm ready for bed. Don't stay up too late."

"I won't." I give Mom a good night kiss. (Giving your mother a good night kiss is totally punk rock, and don't you forget it!) And then I sit down on the couch. I text with Audrey for a while, giving her the latest thrilling updates, and then I brush my teeth, floss (I don't expect you to consider me as a role model, but, yes, I floss every day), take care of other business that doesn't require a detailed description, and then head to my bedroom.

(Okay, you need to trust me as a narrator, so I'll confess

that I don't floss *every* day. But I floss at least three days out of five. That's a sixty percent flossing rate. When the dentist asks, I lie and say that I floss every day, but it's not like I'm saying, "Yep, I'm a flosser!" while plant life grows between my molars. I do have the occasional cavity. So though I'm not a perfect role model for dental hygiene, I do all right. And if you're one of those people who thinks, *Gosh, yanking strings around my teeth sure seems like a lot of work!* I hope you'll consider shifting your point of view and say, "Rod Conklin, lead singer of Fanged Grapefruit, flosses an adequate amount and now I shall too!")

(I apologize if you're not the kind of person who enjoys long parenthetical digressions. I'll try to do better in future chapters, although I make no promises.)

(Note that I said *future* chapters. This chapter is going to be all parenthetical digressions, all the time! Woo!)

(Okay, I've got that out of my system. Apologies. But I can't offer a refund for the purchase price of that portion of the book.)

As I open my bedroom door, it creaks. Fortunately, the creak is not nearly as loud as Blake's awe-inspiring snoring, so I don't wake him up.

It's dark in my room, but something seems wrong.

The first wrong thing is that Blake is sleeping in my bed

instead of on the inflatable mattress that I set up for him. But that doesn't surprise me at all. Something else disturbs me.

I turn on the light.

Blake has redecorated my room.

To be fair, he's only redecorated half of it. But he's taken down everything on the left side of the room and replaced it with his own stuff. The punk rock band posters and a *Guitars through History* calendar that I'd had on my wall now rest in a neat stack on my desk.

I really don't like the idea of Blake messing with my posters. He'd better not have torn any corners. If he's so much as *crinkled* one of them, oh, how my cousin will suffer! Death would be too good for him!

The left side of my room is now decorated, walls and ceiling, with animal pictures. But not cute animals (I can enjoy a kitten picture as much as anybody) and not interesting animals (giraffes sure have wacky necks!) and not majestic animals (lions, tigers, elephants, pumas, leopards, hippos, etc.) and not even animals that indicate some sort of hobby. (For example, I don't necessarily want to spend every evening looking at a picture of a salmon, but at least I could say, "Okay, Blake enjoys fishing.")

No, Cousin Blake seems to have a thing for rodents.

I'm serious. There are pictures of rats, squirrels, opossums, and lemmings. If it's got beady eyes and fur, there's a picture of it up on my wall. Why would anybody want to look at a squirrel on purpose?

The giant-sized poster of a rat on my ceiling looks like it's in 3-D. It's not a greasy sewer rat, but it's still a rat that's placed exactly where I stare at the ceiling when I can't fall asleep. If I already can't sleep, how is a three-foot-long rat going to improve the situation?

Blake rolls over on his side. "Too much light," he mutters.

"I didn't give you permission to do this," I whisper.

Blake opens one eye. "Huh?"

"Nobody said you could mess with my stuff."

"I only touched my half of the room."

"It's not *your* half of the room. It's my room, and I'm letting you stay here. You don't get to change it around without asking."

"Why didn't you say something earlier?"

"I didn't think anything needed to be said!"

"Bad call on your part."

"You don't take down my posters without telling me. That's totally uncool, and I'm pretty sure you know it."

"Am I supposed to feel like I'm in a museum here?"

"No, but you're supposed to ask permission before redecorating."

"Hmm."

"Could you open your other eye while we talk?"

Blake opens his other eye and sits up in bed. "I apologize for not knowing that you were my all-powerful ruler. I assumed that since we were sharing this living space, I'd be allowed to make a small effort to stave off the homesickness and make myself at home."

"Don't say stave. Nobody says stave."

"I say stave several times a day."

"No, you don't."

"Whatever."

"How would you feel if I went into your room and took down your rodent posters?" I ask.

"Please don't call them rodents. It's disrespectful."

"No, it's not. That's what they're called."

"If you say so."

"It's the actual word! Rodents! It's not a derogatory term! It's like calling cats felines!"

"Since you're my ruler, I guess I can't argue."

"Are you kidding me?" I know that there is a zero percent chance that this conversation is worth continuing, yet for some strange reason, I forge onward. "If I told somebody they had a rodent face, yeah, that would be disrespectful. But calling a rat a rodent is just using the proper term."

"Did you really wake me up to discuss animal classifications?" Blake asks.

"No, I woke you up because you took down my posters."

"Your posters weren't injured."

"That's not the point."

"What is the point?"

"The point is that we're not roommates. You're a guest. I'm totally willing to compromise. I even cleaned up my room for you, which is something I never do. But if you want to change things around, we have to discuss it first. That's all."

"We'll just have to agree to disagree."

"No! I don't agree to that!"

"Rodney, Rodney, Rodney," says Blake. "You need to relax. Being so high-strung isn't good for you. You don't want to have a nervous breakdown, do you?"

"I'd rather not, no."

"So take a deep breath. In the grand scope of the universe in which we live, the posters in your room are a mere speck on a dot. In the overall scheme of things, it wouldn't even matter if I set them on fire."

Did my cousin threaten to set my posters on fire, or is he trying to make a point? The fact that I'm not immediately sure is a little scary.

"All I'm saying is—" I begin.

"You don't need to say anything. You've made your point. If I'd known you had a squirrel phobia, I never would have decorated my half of the room this way. I'll take them down first thing in the morning, unless they're going to give you nightmares."

There's a pillow nearby that looks like it could be an excellent smothering tool. That's probably a bad idea.

Sure, I could explain that I don't have a squirrel phobia, but then he'd say something else infuriating, and we'd go back and forth until I start to gnaw off my own lips. For my own sanity, it's time to bail.

"Good night, Blake," I say.

"Good night, Rodney."

"Call me Rodney again, and I'll shave off your eyebrows while you sleep."

"Good night, Rod."

"Good night."

Only ninety-two more days to go.

7.

SO I THINK Cousin Blake may be evil," I tell Mom in the morning.

"Excuse me?"

"He's evil. I'm not saying that he'd push somebody in front of a bus—though I'm not ruling that out—but I think there's something genuinely wrong with him...in an evilish kind of way."

Mom stops pouring her cup of coffee. "What makes you say that?"

"Basically, it was all the evil things he said and did yesterday."

"Rod..."

"I'm not asking you to talk to him about it," I say. "I can handle the situation. I just want it on record that I think he's pure, dark evil."

Mom resumes pouring her coffee. "Noted, I guess."

Blake is still asleep. I had to play loud music through

my headphones and put several layers of blanket over my head to drown out his snoring last night. If this continues, those layers of blanket are going to be stuffed in his mouth. Though prison wouldn't be fun, at least it would be quieter.

"Like I said, I can handle it, but he should have come with a warning label."

"It's natural for there to be an adjustment period," says Mom. "You've never had to share your space like this before. You're used to having things your own way."

"No, no, no, no, no, this isn't me being selfish," I insist. "I'm the good cousin here. He's…he's rotten. We'll work it out, but I'll tell you right now, for the sake of my social standing, I'm going to pretend I don't know him tomorrow at school."

"I hope you change your mind."

"Not likely, but we'll see." It hasn't even been twenty-four hours. Blake could still be a cool guy. Maybe his ears didn't properly pop during the flight.

Mom heads off to work. Everybody is going to come over for band practice this afternoon, so we've got to get Blake's boxes out of the garage, but I'm not going to touch them until Blake is up to do his share. Until Blake is awake…until Blake, that snake, is awake to take a break from being a flake and make my garage… Sorry, I'm not good at making up song lyrics on the spot. He doesn't deserve his own song anyway.

Around noon, the snoring ceases. He's either awake or dead. Despite the impression I may have given, I hope it's the former.

My bedroom door opens and Blake emerges, looking like somebody who's stepped off a thirty-six-hour ride on a Tilt-A-Whirl. "G'mrn," he says, which I think translates to "Good morning."

"Good morning, Sunshine," I tell him. "I trust you had a restful night?"

"It was okay. Mattress could be better."

"Well, it'll be a lot better tonight because you'll be sleeping on the air mattress."

Blake scowls. "Ugh, no, I don't do air mattresses."

"Sure, you do. I blew it up all by myself. You don't want to hurt my feelings, do you? It took forever."

"You didn't use a pump?"

"Nope. We don't have one. That's all my carbon dioxide in there. Will you be enjoying a refreshing shower before you dine?"

"You don't have a bathtub?"

I shake my head. "Sorry."

"So I have to stand?"

"Yes."

"Who doesn't have a bathtub?"

I raise my hand. "Me. It's inconvenient, I know. But water spraying on you is just as useful as water that you sit in. Actually, it's better because the grime isn't floating around you while you're trying to get clean. If you'd like to order an outdoor pool, be my guest."

Blake glares at me and wanders into the bathroom.

A few minutes later, he emerges, hair wet and a towel wrapped around his waist. "Have a nice shower?" I ask.

"Yeah, whatever."

"Did you figure out that the red arrow on the knob was for hot water and the blue arrow was for cold? I know it can be difficult since water that comes out of the faucet is clear."

Blake ignores me and walks into my bedroom. If we're trying to mend our relationship, I suppose I should stop being sarcastic.

When he comes back out, he's fully dressed. "I still can't believe you don't have a bathtub."

"We don't have rubber duckies either." Okay, I'll stop being sarcastic *now*.

"Showers are for hosing yourself down after you've run a marathon," says Blake. "It's a low-class way to get clean."

"That's an interesting new perspective." New plan: I'm

not going to stop being sarcastic until he stops complaining about our lack of a bathtub.

"Bathtubs are elegant. They're relaxing."

"You just woke up. You don't need extra relaxation. But here's what we're going to do. We'll go out and buy some shovels. Then we'll dig a great big hole in the backyard, which you can fill with hot water and bubbles, and then—"

"Ha ha. That's hilarious."

"Thank you," I say. "I spent almost twenty seconds thinking it up. I didn't originally have the bubbles part in there, but that's what makes the joke, don't you agree?"

"What's for breakfast?"

"It's lunchtime."

"I don't eat lunch before breakfast."

"There's cold cereal then."

"Oh, joy."

"You don't like cereal?"

"I outgrew cereal when I outgrew cartoons."

"But maybe you'll find a toy car in the box. Vroom, vroom."

"I really don't understand you," says Blake. "Immaturity is fine when you're younger, but you should be over it."

"For your information, we have only healthy cereal in the cupboard. Maybe it's because I've outgrown cereals with prizes inside, and maybe it's because I love raisins. You'll never know."

"Raisins are old grapes."

"We're not going to get off on a raisin tangent," I inform him. "I'm actually a very good breakfast chef. I can make pancakes, waffles, omelets, perfectly crisp bacon, and though I don't make my own jelly, I spread it across toast with skill beyond anything you've never seen. And someday in the future, I might make this for you. Until that day arrives, it's cold cereal for you."

"I didn't ask you to make breakfast for me," says Blake.

I think back. I'm pretty sure he did. I hope he did. My whole dramatic speech only works if Blake is too lazy to cook his own breakfast.

"I can make light and fluffy blueberry pancakes that will bring a tear to your eye," says Blake. "My elevated take on waffles would start your day on such a high note that nothing could ruin it. Omelets are my specialty, especially the ones I make with perfectly crisp bacon. And I *do* make my own jelly."

I'm almost positive he's lying. He was convincing until he got to the part about making his own jelly. Blake seems to be the kind of person who would ridicule homemade jelly, not make it himself. But if I call him out, I run the risk of him proving me wrong by making us a delicious breakfast, and then I'll look like a jerk.

I decide to call his bluff. "I'll happily drive you to the store for eggs and jelly-making supplies if you want."

"No need. I'll have toast."

I show him where we keep the bread, and he drops two slices into the toaster. I silently dare him to criticize our toaster. *Go on, Blake. Say that our toaster isn't up to contemporary standards. You know you want to. Talk about how your toaster at home has four slots or how ours doesn't have a sturdy enough spring or how the sides could stand to be a bit shinier. Do it. I dare you. Do it. Do it!*

Blake says nothing.

The toast pops up. It's burnt.

"Oh, yeah," I say, avoiding eye contact. "The settings aren't quite right. Our toaster is extra hot. If you want it toasted at six, you have to set it for four. Sorry about that."

"Most people would have shared that information sooner," Blake comments.

"I know, I know." I was so focused on the possibility of Blake making fun of our toaster that I forgot that this appliance's glory days are long gone.

I take the burnt toast from him, throw it in the garbage, and give him two new slices of bread.

"You didn't have to waste it," Blake says. "I would've scraped off the burnt layers and eaten my paper-thin pieces of toast without complaining."

"Set it at four," I remind him.

Blake turns the dial. "You should get a dog."

"Why?"

"To eat all the food you ruin."

"I don't generally ruin food."

"Well, so far you're zero for one. I guess we'll see how the rest of my visit goes. I don't want to have to buy pizza for every meal, even though I can afford it." Blake puts the bread in the toaster and pushes down the lever. "You're sure it should be set on four, right? You're not second-guessing yourself?"

I want to come back with a devastating retort, but I did botch the toast, so for now, I have to endure his sarcasm. "I'm sure."

"I suppose we'll know in a minute."

It's extremely frustrating to feel like he's winning this battle over toast. I should be winning the toast battles in my own home.

"We have to talk about some things," I say.

"Ooh, that sounds like fun."

"I'll sleep on the inflatable mattress, and you can keep up

65

your posters. All I ask is that we discuss stuff like this ahead of time. You can't just assume that you get my bed."

"I can't?"

"No."

"Hmm."

"Stop saying hmm."

"Does it bother you?"

"Yes."

"You must have a pretty low threshold if that bothers you, huh?"

"No," I say. "Until you got here, I was known for being casual and easygoing, except onstage. But you're trying to mess up my life."

"Would you say I'm turning your life topsy-turvy? Or is it more helter-skelter?"

My jaw drops. Because this seems to be an admission that he's behaving like this on purpose, rather than simply being oblivious to his inner creep. Is he trying to get sent home for bad behavior?

Blake must notice my shock. He smiles. "We keep getting off on the wrong foot, don't we?"

"Yeah."

"We're going to run out of feet."

"Probably."

"I'm sorry I stole your bed. I don't want to be ungrateful to your lungs. I'll use the air mattress. Make sure you change your sheets though. I sweat a lot while I sleep."

"You can keep the bed. It's okay."

"And I'll take down my posters."

"The posters are fine."

"I'll ask permission before I do anything else disruptive," says Blake. "I get where you're coming from. Your room is sacred. Anything else?"

"No, that's pretty much it."

"Good. Where's the jelly?"

"In the refrigerator."

Blake opens the refrigerator. He takes out all three jars of jelly and sets them on the counter.

"Oh, one more thing," I say. "My band uses the garage to practice, but it's filled with all your boxes. Any chance you could go through them, get the stuff you really need, and put the rest in storage?"

Blake nods. "Absolutely. If I rent a truck, will you help me load half of the boxes?"

"Of course."

"Thanks, Rod. Now, I don't mean to be rude, but I can't talk and put jelly on my toast at the same time."

I want to say, *Really?* But we're on the road to repairing

our relationship, and I don't want to goof it up. I watch as Blake very slowly spreads grape, strawberry, and blackberry jelly on his toast, three perfect lengthwise stripes per slice. Even for somebody like me who takes his peanut butter very seriously, this is weird. The careful application of spreads must be a family trait.

If he's trying to get along with me, Blake can apply sixteen flavors of jelly in a quilt pattern for all I care, but I'm not convinced he's being genuine. I'm going to have to stay on high alert around my cousin. If he's been this frustrating already, there's no telling how awful he can be if he sets his mind to it.

8.

YOU KNOW WHO I really don't like? My cousin Blake.

This isn't new information to those of you who've been dutifully reading along, but I thought a recap would be nice for those of you who might be joining us in the eighth chapter or who put the book aside for a while and are just now resuming the adventures of Rod Conklin and his cousin, Blake Montgomery.

"But weren't things starting to look up at the end of the last chapter?" you might ask. Yes, they were. Oh, sure, I was a bit suspicious, but there was the possibility that he'd seen the error of his ways and that the rest of this book would be a lighthearted recap of our amazing exploits as the best of friends. *And then we bought cotton candy, and Blake got some stuck on his chin. And we laughed and laughed and laughed!*

Instead I'm loading boxes into the back of a truck.

"Um, okay," you're probably saying. "Loading boxes into the back of a truck is nobody's idea of a good time, but if I remember correctly, Blake said he'd rent a truck to clear the garage for band practice if you'd help load half of the boxes. And you agreed. What's the problem? Did he make you load *all* the boxes?"

No.

"Did he make you load all the heavy ones?"

No.

"Then what's the deal? I'm not the one writing this book, so you can't expect me to tell the story for you!"

Fair enough. Here's what happened.

A U-Haul pulls into my driveway. I open the garage door as the driver (not the same one as before, although if somebody makes a movie version of this novel, they're welcome to combine them into one character so they only have to cast one actor) gets out of the truck.

"Mr. Montgomery?" he asks.

"That's me," says Blake. He gestures to the boxes that fill my garage. "It's all of these, but you only need to load half. My cousin's going to carry the rest."

That, ladies and gentlemen, is why I'm not fond of my cousin.

Yes, Blake sits in a lawn chair watching as the driver and I load the (not light) boxes into the back of the truck. What am I supposed to do? Refuse? I need the room in my garage.

Trust me—I glare at Blake every time I pick up a new box with all the fury my eyebrows can summon.

Blake grins and sips his lemonade.

"What's in these boxes?" asks the driver, breathing heavy from the effort of lifting them.

"Blocks of steel," Blake replies. He chuckles, but I'm not sure he's kidding.

We eventually finish, and the driver heads off to the storage facility. It's worth noting that Blake didn't open a single one. It seems paranoid to suggest that the only reason he shipped these boxes to Florida was to mess with me, so I won't suggest that. I don't want you to think I'm paranoid.

Blake slurps up the last of his lemonade and then holds the glass out to me. "Refill?"

"Are you kidding me?"

"I didn't mean that you should make a special trip. I figured you were heading inside anyway."

"I am, but I'm not getting you more lemonade."

Blake sucks some air through the straw since there's no liquid left to slurp. "Is there a problem?" he asks.

"Gosh, I don't know. Maybe it's—"

"Didn't you agree to load half of the boxes?"

"Yes, I did."

"Did you have to load *more* than half of them?"

"No."

"Me paying somebody else to do my half didn't create any extra work for you. I don't see why you're upset."

Credit where it's due. Blake is a very good actor. He knows perfectly well why I'm upset, but if somebody were standing around listening to our conversation, that person might think he was being genuine. They might think I was the bad guy for picturing running over him with my car.

"You know exactly what you're doing," I inform him.

"I didn't realize that carrying boxes was so traumatic for you. I assumed that guitar players had strong arms."

"I have amazing arms! I'll load boxes all day, no problem. But I don't like doing it when they're your boxes and you're being lazy."

"Lazy…or smart?"

"Lazy."

"Or smart?"

"Lazy," I say definitively.

"Look," says Blake, "I'll be the first to admit that my arms weren't designed for lifting things. If I've got the money, why shouldn't I pay somebody to do the work for me?"

"Don't play dumb."

"Are you mad because you weren't paid? I figured that since we're family, it would be inappropriate to offer to compensate you. But here." He holds his empty glass toward me. "I'll give you a buck to get me another glass of lemonade."

Not gonna lie. It would be an easy dollar. But I'm not going to play his game.

I turn away from him and walk into the garage.

"Fine. A buck fifty. Do you take plastic? I can start a tab. We'll settle up when I leave."

I turn around. "Like I said, this isn't going to continue."

"I'm trying to generate some income for you, Rod. Most people in your position would be delighted to get me a refill on my lemonade."

"I'll tell my mom that I don't want you to stay here anymore," I answer. "Your parents can cut their stupid cruise short and pick up their bratty son. Or you can fly back to California and stay by yourself. You're sixteen. Why do you need us to babysit you anyway?"

I may have struck a nerve. "You're not my babysitter," he says.

"Then stop acting like a baby."

"Babies don't hire people."

"Apparently, they do."

"You got outsmarted. Get over it."

Outsmarted? *Outsmarted?* Can you believe what you're reading?

"I think we have very different definitions of what it

means to outsmart somebody," I say. "You didn't do anything clever. If a dog has an accident on the kitchen floor and you have to clean it up, that dog didn't outsmart you."

"Very well," says Blake, standing. "No dollar fifty for you. I would've gone as high as a buck seventy-five, but you've lost out."

"I'm not impressed that you have spending money. Don't act like you're an entrepreneur because you get an allowance."

"Ooh, look at Rodney's fancy words!"

"Entrepreneur? That's a normal word. And you can't look at my words. You're listening to them."

"Whatever."

(I realize that you, as the reader of this book, are indeed looking at my words, unless you're listening to it on audiobook or somebody is reading it out loud. But I was talking to Blake. Sorry if there was confusion.)

"All I'm saying, Blake, is don't get too comfortable."

Blake sits back down. He sets the empty glass on the ground and then stretches out his legs and puts his arms up over his head, getting comfortable.

"Like this?" he asks.

"Yeah, like that."

"I'd hate to have to tell my parents that you were being a poor host."

"What are they going to do, not send me a birthday card?"

"For starters."

"It's adorable that you think I'm scared of Aunt Mary and Uncle Clark. Oh, don't get me wrong, I still remember when Aunt Mary made me stand in the corner for ten minutes for not wiping my feet before I came inside. If they put me in time-out, I'll have to take it like a man."

"Do you know what I'd advise?" Blake asks.

"Nope. Not a clue. What would you advise?"

"I'd advise you to stop pretending you're not scared of me."

"What?"

"You heard me."

"I can't possibly have heard you correctly. Because what I heard is you saying that I'm scared of you."

"Then you heard right. Go ahead and deny it if you want."

"That's not even worth denying. It would be like me insisting that I'm not really Iron Man."

"Say what you will. We both know the truth."

I shake my head. "You're trying to draw me into one of those conversations that makes me want to rip out my hair. Not gonna happen. My hair is one of my best features."

"Hi, Rod!" says Audrey.

I spin around. Audrey rides her bicycle up my driveway. She always lets me know before she comes over, but I've been too busy loading boxes and dealing with Cousin Satan to pay attention to my phone.

"Oh, hi," I say, trying to pretend that I'm happy to see my girlfriend. I'd warned her about Blake, but seeing him in action might cause her to question my DNA. Maybe I should tell her he was adopted. In fact, I'll say that we were both adopted to distance our bloodlines even further.

I wonder if Audrey will get to meet Good Blake or Evil Blake. I'm not sure which will be better for me.

"You didn't answer your texts, but I didn't think you'd mind me coming over."

"It's great to see you."

Audrey gets off her bike and puts down the kickstand. Blake is staring at her the way a guy does when he's not used to being in the presence of attractive women. If I could read his thoughts, I'm sure they'd be *Duurrrr derp durrrr durr derp*.

She walks over to Blake. "Hi," she says. "I'm Audrey."

"I'm…Cousin."

"Nice to meet you, Cousin."

"Blake."

"Cousin Blake, right. Rod told me all about you."

Blake opens his mouth as if to speak, but no sound emerges. A trickle of sweat runs down his forehead.

"Yes, this is Blake," I say. "He was just offering me a dollar fifty to get him a glass of lemonade."

"I'll do it for a dollar and a quarter," says Audrey with a smile. "So what've you guys been doing?"

"I've been loading half of those boxes into a truck to be taken to storage, while Blake here paid somebody to move the other half. You sure can't accuse him of worrying too much about what other people think of him."

Audrey frowns at me. "Be nice."

"I'm at maximum niceness," I say. "Hey, Audrey, you look parched from your bike ride. Would you care for a glass of cold, refreshing lemonade?"

She continues to frown at me. If anybody deserves frowns, it's Blake. But she hasn't seen that I'm justified in being extremely rude.

"I'd love a drink," she says. "Can I get you something, Blake?"

Blake opens his mouth again but still doesn't speak any words with success. I'm pretty sure he's fallen madly in love with her. Too bad for him. I win this round.

9.

BLAKE NEVER DID successfully communicate whether he'd like Audrey to get him another glass of lemonade, though I think she took his slack-jawed silence as a yes. As we walk inside my house, she frowns at me yet again.

"What's your deal?" she asks.

"What's *my* deal?"

"That's whose deal I was asking about, yes."

"Were you not listening to our conversation last night? He's like some mad scientist's experiment to create the world's worst human being."

"That's no excuse for your behavior. This isn't like you," says Audrey.

"That's because my usual personality was developed by *not* being around Blake. I guarantee that if you're around him for long, you'll become three hundred percent ruder too."

"Maybe. But he just arrived. You should try to work things out."

I shudder. "Those are the most chilling words you've ever said. And I totally get what you're saying. I've tried to be nice, but he is awful back."

"Why would he want this to be awful?"

"I don't know! The workings of his mind would require an army of psychologists to figure out! Half of them would run away screaming! The dude doesn't make any sense."

"Do you want me to beat him up for you?"

"Yes, please."

Audrey grins. "That was a joke. All I'm saying is…don't make this harder for yourself."

"I won't," I say. "Maybe he lives in a place where wild chimpanzees are always jumping down on him from the trees and clawing at his head, and now that he's in a chimpanzee-free zone, he's so confused that he doesn't know how to behave."

"That must be it." Audrey rolls her eyes.

"Unless he's, y'know, the devil."

"I feel like the devil would have higher aspirations."

"I'd think so too, but who are we to judge?"

I pour Audrey a glass of lemonade.

"Are you going to let me bring him one?" she asks.

"I'd rather you didn't."

"I'm completely on your side, but maybe a peace offering from me will help smooth things over."

"It'll probably make him jealous. 'Argh! She's beautiful and smart *and* she brings lemonade to guests? I can't handle it! I can't handle it!'" I wish I could say that I did a dead-on impression of Blake, but it's actually not very good.

"I'll go out on a limb and say that me bringing him lemonade will not send him spiraling into jealousy over our relationship."

"I dunno," I say. "On a scale of one to ten, how would you rank his verbal abilities after he saw you?"

"Three. He did eventually produce sound."

"He was entranced. Which you should definitely take as a compliment, but watch that he doesn't try to steal locks of your hair."

Audrey takes a drink. "Is he gonna get suspicious that it's taking us so long?"

"Maybe. I don't really see him as a 'get up to investigate' kind of guy. He's more like a Sherlock Holmes who waits for the criminals to walk into his office and confess."

"You did say he took down all your posters and put up his own. That's not lazy."

I shrug. "Fair enough. But I'm not incorporating him into my social life. He's going to be like Neptune's moons. You know they exist, but they aren't an important part of your daily life."

"Neptune has fourteen moons," says Audrey.

"Fourteen?" That Audrey knows this is another reason why my girlfriend is awesome…even if it sorta disproves my point.

"Despina, Galatea, Halimede, Laomedeia, Larissa, Naiad, Nereid, Neso, Proteus, Psamathe, S/2004 N 1, Sao, Triton, and Thalassa."

"Did you do those in alphabetical order?"

"Yes."

"How did I not know that you could rattle off all fourteen of Neptune's moons in alphabetical order?"

"I don't do it very often."

"Wow. We need to use those in a song."

"They're hard to rhyme."

In case you think I'm an inattentive boyfriend, I knew that Audrey was really intelligent and that she had a head for facts and figures. I didn't realize she was an astronomy wizard too. We've only been together for about three months, which may be why I am always learning new details about her. I don't think I shared that timeline before. I didn't want to overwhelm you with exposition too early, but it's possible that backfired and you thought we'd known each other since kindergarten, in which case I definitely should've known that she could name all fourteen moons. Remind me when we get to a slow part, and I'll do a flashback about how we met.

"I forgot how we got on this subject," I say.

"You were saying that eventually, you wouldn't remember if Blake exists or not."

"Right. He'll be like *Home Alone 5*. Was there a *Home Alone 5*? Maybe, maybe not. Somebody has to know, but it's not me."

"I have no idea how many *Home Alone* sequels there were," says Audrey.

"Then it's a perfect metaphor."

"Okay, I won't bring him lemonade."

"Good. I'm not trying to deprive him. He can have all he wants. He can drink lemonade until he looks like a giant yellow balloon. He just has to get it himself."

"That's reasonable."

"Do you want to see a neat trick?" I say.

"Sure."

"All we have to do is stay inside. He'll sit out there until he's dying of thirst before he gets his own lemonade. It'll be funny!"

"It sounds mean," says Audrey.

"If letting my cousin dehydrate is mean, I don't want to be nice."

"Actually, based on what you've said, he'll have it delivered. We'll go back out there and he'll be sipping a frosty beverage with a paper umbrella that makes what we're drinking look like bathtub water."

"Blake's a fan of bathtub water."

"Drinking it?"

"No. I mean, I hope not. Ew. Why did you put that image in my head? I thought you cared about me."

"I think you're thinking about this way too much," says Audrey.

She may be right. You can definitely make an argument that I'm pettier than I was twenty-four hours ago. (Did he really just get here yesterday? Feels like it was seventeen years ago, and I'm only sixteen.)

"Yeah, I probably am," I admit. "But watch. He won't come in and refill his own glass under any—"

The door to the garage opens, and Blake walks into the kitchen. "Hi," he says, going over to the refrigerator. He takes out the pitcher of lemonade, and he refills his glass. He takes a long drink and then pours more to top it off. "Mmm, delicious," he says, putting the pitcher back in the refrigerator.

It's definitely in the top five most frustrating times I've watched somebody pour themselves a drink.

"See you guys outside," says Blake, leaving with a wave.

"He did that on purpose," I tell Audrey. "You think I'm wrong?"

"I mean, uh, I don't think he poured the lemonade on accident."

"He knew I'd tell you that he wouldn't do it, so he did it to make me look stupid."

"Maybe."

"Not maybe. Definitely. He knew I was in here saying that he was a jerk, so he behaved like a normal person on purpose. Now I look like the jerk. I look unhinged, right?"

"A little."

"See?"

"Do you think it's possible that—and bear with me on this line of logic—he was simply thirsty?"

"I know he was thirsty! What I'm saying is that…"

I trail off because I realize that I will not look back on this conversation with pride. If I want to keep Audrey as my girlfriend for more than three months, I need to calm down.

"Sorry," I say. "I was on an inflatable mattress, and I didn't sleep very well."

"Why did you get the—"

"Doesn't matter."

I can't let Blake turn me into a twitchy person. That's his role, not mine. I'm a well-adjusted kid who works out his problems through his music.

The door to the garage opens again, and Blake walks back

into the kitchen, holding an empty glass. "There's nothing better than a cold glass of lemonade on a hot day, am I right?"

"You're right," I say.

"This was freshly squeezed, wasn't it?"

"Nope. Powder."

"Well, whoever added the water and stirred really knew what they were doing. Nobody likes gritty lemonade."

Audrey giggles. I think she mistook his obnoxious comment for an attempt to be amusing.

Blake pours himself another glass. "How long have you two known each other?" he asks.

"Three months," says Audrey. (Okay, I guess I didn't need the exposition earlier in the chapter.)

Blake nods his approval. "That's an exciting time in a relationship."

I'm pretty sure that the closest Blake has ever come to a romantic relationship involves awkward conversations with girls over the punch bowl at school dances, but I don't say anything.

Audrey puts her arm around me. "Nonstop excitement."

Wait. Was she being ironic? Surely, she wasn't being ironic. Her tone sounded slightly ironic, but I must have misheard. No way was she being ironic.

"I can tell by the vibe between you two that you're perfect

for each other," says Blake. He chuckles. "I look forward to my wedding invitation."

Audrey also chuckles.

I do not chuckle.

"Rod said you were great, and I totally see it. You two make sense. You *fit*."

"Well, thank you," says Audrey. "I agree." She gives my shoulders a squeeze.

He's not looking at her in a creepy manner or anything, but still, I don't like Blake complimenting my relationship with my girlfriend. I'm ready for him to go back outside now.

"I hear that Fanged Grapefruit is amazing," says Blake. "I can't wait to be in the front row at their next show."

"There isn't actual seating," I say.

"Standing up front then."

"Sorry," Audrey tells Blake. "He's being pedantic."

One thing I like less than Blake complimenting my relationship with my girlfriend is my girlfriend apologizing to Blake for my being pedantic, even if I was. Next she'll say she's attracted to guys who have posters of rats on their walls.

I want to make sure that Blake knows he isn't welcome at a Fanged Grapefruit show, but this is not the time. Instead I smile politely. (Which is difficult. My face really doesn't want to contort into a smile right now. It takes a lot of muscle control to make it happen.)

The two of them keep talking and laughing. I consider it a personal victory that I don't throw back my head and let out a bellow of primal anguish. Why am I the only one who can see the real Blake?

10.

WOW. CHAPTER TEN. I honestly thought I'd have a nervous breakdown before we got here.

I can't bring myself to provide a transcript of Audrey and Blake's conversation in the kitchen, but let's just say they got along perfectly well. It's not like I started to think he was going to steal my woman, but I guess I'd hoped she'd dislike him as much as I do.

The torture ends when Mel and Clarissa arrive. (Recap: Mel = lead guitar. Clarissa = drums.) Clarissa's mom is heavily tattooed and has several face piercings, so it's always odd to see her drive up in a minivan with four kids in the back. I help Clarissa unpack her drums. If Blake offers to assist, I will bash a cymbal over my head, but he doesn't.

I introduce Mel and Clarissa to Blake. They're both considerate enough to look like they don't really want to meet him, though that could be my wishful thinking.

We set up in the garage. Blake goes inside the house,

which makes me happy, but then he comes back out, which makes me sad. He sits back down in the lawn chair. There's a notebook on his lap. I do not know its purpose. I assume I will not like it.

"Mind if I watch you guys practice?" asks Blake.

Mel and Clarissa shrug. Okay, fine. Audrey is hanging out to hear us play. Blake's welcome to watch as long as he doesn't interrupt.

"Go ahead," I say. "I'll warn you right now. We're noisy."

"Yeah, we are!" says Mel with pride. "Noisiest band in the state!"

"Scoot your chair into the garage," I tell Blake. "I have to close the door so the neighbors won't complain."

"And so we don't shatter windows for a six-block radius," adds Clarissa.

We have never actually shattered a window, except for one time when a drumstick flew out of Clarissa's hand, but we like to think of our music as being so intense that it could generate a giant sinkhole if we don't take proper precautions.

"Sounds amazing," says Blake, bringing the lawn chair into the garage. He sits down again as I press the button. The garage door closes like a curtain. That's right. Fanged Grapefruit rocks so hard that the curtain closes instead of opens before we begin playing. For the safety of the audience, of course.

The bottom of the garage door hits the cement with the sound of thunder (in our minds).

"Which song first?" asks Mel.

"How about 'Poison-Tipped Daffodil Man?'" I suggest.

I count us down, and then we launch into the song, which goes:

He's a poison-tipped daffodil man!
A poison-tipped daffodil man!
A poison-tipped daffodil man!
Better not give him a hug!

There are eight more verses, all with similar impact. Ma Conklin didn't raise no braggart, but trust me, we sound amazing.

"'The Night I Drank Way Too Many Blue Raspberry Slushes,'" Clarissa suggests.

"*Last night!*" I sing.

"*A bad night!*" Mel and Clarissa sing.

"*I said last night!*"

"*A very bad night!*"

"*I drank one!*"

"*One!*"

"*Two!*"

"*Two!*"

"*Three!*"

"*Three!*"

"*Four and five!*"

"*Four and five!*"

"*Six, seven, and eight!*"

"*Six, seven, and eight!*"

"*Nine, ten, eleven, twelve!*"

"*Nine, ten, eleven, twelve!*"

"*I drank twelve blue raspberry slushes!*"

"*Twelve slushes!*"

"*And then I drank one more!*"

"*One more!*"

"*And I realized,*" I sing. "*Oh yeah, I realized.*"

"*He realized. Oh yeah, he realized,*" Mel and Clarissa sing the chorus.

"*I realized, just last night that thirteen—yeah, thirteen—thirteen blue raspberry slushes...*" Big finish here. "*...was too many blue raspberry slushies to drink!*"

At an actual performance, we stick out our tongues to show that they're all blue, but there's no reason to do that in rehearsal.

Mel and Clarissa's harmonizing was off a bit, so we do that one again. Then we switch to "I Love You So Much I'd Blow

Up the Moon." We're still tweaking the lyrics on that song, but it's the tender story of a girl whose love for a boy is so strong that she'd destroy a celestial body for him if he asked. He does ask. In the end, the girl learns that (A) it's extremely difficult to blow up the moon, and (B) if a boy asks you to destroy the moon to earn his love, he's not worth the trouble. We have to rework the lyrics because, after all, she *did* make the offer in the first place, so our theme is a bit muddled.

We're also still adjusting the melody and arrangement, so we go through it several times, stopping and restarting, altering our performance each time. Blake is busy writing in his notebook.

We spend about half an hour on this song. We're not one hundred percent satisfied with the results by the end, but we all agree that it's time to move on to "Godzilla Burned My Yoga Pants." We've got that one down pretty well. Then it's on to "Mr. Dentist, Drill My Teeth but Leave the Rest of My Skull Alone." (My mom doesn't like this song. It's not autobiographical. As I've mentioned before, I floss and have good oral hygiene, so I haven't had a lot of cavities.) During this song we play the prerecorded sound of a whirring dentist drill in the background, which makes the audience cringe, but that's why we're punk rock and not gospel.

If we can get a dentist drill cheap, we'll have Audrey run

around onstage with it, looking scary, but so far we haven't been able to find one.

Blake is still writing in his notebook. Since his mouth remains closed, we're cool.

We go through "Don't Eat Meat Unless It's in Cow Form," "Checkmate, Checkmate, Checkmate," "That Spider Just Hissed at Me," "I Ain't Doing My Homework Tonight (Because I Did It This Afternoon)," and everybody's favorite, "Thud Thump Crash Crunch Splat Squish."

By the end, we're drenched with perspiration and feeling great. All my problems have vanished. Audrey claps and grins at our performance. I don't even care about Blake anymore.

Blake stands up.

He applauds. "Great job, you guys. I assumed you were talented performers, but this exceeded my expectations. In every major category that I could judge a musical act, you were top-notch."

"Thanks, dude," says Mel. "I appreciate it."

"Yeah, thanks," says Clarissa. She tosses him one of her pulverized drumsticks.

"When's your next jig?"

"Gig?" Mel asks.

Blake chuckles. "Yes, gig. Sorry. I got confused because your music made me want to dance a jig."

Everybody except me laughs.

"We play every Monday night at the Lane," I tell him.

"Is it a nice place?"

"No. It's the opposite of that."

"I guess you wouldn't want to play in an opera house." This doesn't get as big of a laugh as his gig/jig joke, but I'm sensing a distinct lack of negativity toward my cousin from my bandmates.

I push the button to open the garage door. Everybody sighs happily as the cool air hits.

"Anyway," says Blake, "I was taking some notes during your practice session, and I thought—if I'm not being too forward—that you might be interested in some feedback."

I knew it! I knew he was going to do something like this! I let down my guard for a few songs, and this is what happens! He's going to say that our band sucks. I'm going to have to stop Mel and Clarissa from beating him up, and it's going to be a great big mess! Argh!

"What kind of feedback?" asks Clarissa, her eyes narrowing.

Blake glances down at his notes. "The first song. 'Poison-Tipped Daffodil Man.' During the bridge I feel like you could slow down the drums a hair."

"She's not slowing anything down a hair," I say.

"It's your call, obviously. I'm not your manager or anything. But as an audience member, I wasn't quite done being amused by the last line of the verse before you went into this really fast drumming. I think slowing down the beat would make it easier to process what I'd heard."

"Punk rock isn't about giving you time to process stuff," I say. "We're fast and proud."

"You're right. You're right. I'm not suggesting that you should pause the song for a mediation break. I'm only saying that if you let it breathe a smidgen, it allows the audience to better appreciate your brilliance."

"Maybe we should try it that way," suggests Clarissa.

"Now?" I ask.

"Sure, why not?"

"I've already opened the garage door."

"It recloses."

"Do you want to hear the rest of my comments first?" asks Blake.

"Yeah, all right," Mel says without enthusiasm.

"Mel, the slush song. After the bridge, decrescendo the third verse and then crescendo into the final chorus. Again, I'm not trying to step on anybody's toes. I know I'd bristle if you offered constructive criticism about my video game playing. But it's something to consider."

"It's actually not a bad idea," Mel admits.

This cannot be happening. Our rule with Fanged Grapefruit is that there are no egos. Everybody has equal say. We're not going to be one of those bands that breaks up because somebody thinks they're the superstar. But I think it's important to point out that *Blake is not a member of Fanged Grapefruit, and he's an awful human being*! I don't want to listen to anything he has to say, even if it does sound reasonable.

"Let's try it," says Clarissa.

My options at this point are faking a horrific index finger injury that prevents me from pushing the button to close the garage door and then hurriedly making up an excuse for why I can't use my remaining nine fingers to push the button while also coming up with a reason why nobody else can push the button either…or closing the door and incorporating Blake's feedback. (I'm sure there are other options, but none occur to me right now.)

I push the button. I wish Blake would give me a smug look so I could point to him and shout, "See that? He's looking smug!" but he maintains a neutral facial expression as the garage door closes.

We play "Poison-Tipped Daffodil Man," incorporating Blake's suggestion. I'm the first to admit when I'm wrong, so I'll say that…

You know what? I don't want to admit that I'm wrong quite yet. Let me share some unrelated thoughts first.

Ducks aren't scary, but I wouldn't want to walk outside at midnight and find two hundred of them in my yard, each one silently staring at me. I understand why some people hate licorice even if I don't share their view. Never trust a lumberjack who giggles the entire time he's chopping down a tree. Sixty people on a trampoline are too many.

Okay. (Deep breath.) The song is indeed better after Blake's feedback.

"You were right," Clarissa tells him. "Thanks."

We play "The Night I Drank Way Too Many Blue Raspberry Slushes." You're not going to make me say it, are you? You are? Fine. Yes, our slush song is better after making the decrescendo/crescendo changes that Blake suggested. Are you happy?

When practice is over and everybody is pleased that we're now .009 percent better, I open the garage door again. Mel leans over to me.

"I hate to say it," he whispers, "but your cousin is pretty cool."

11.

BLAKE ASKS IF he can come along when I drive everybody home. My personal preference would be for Blake to not accompany us, for reasons I don't think I need to spell out eleven chapters into this tale of woe. But since Clarissa is leaving her drums in my garage until the gig tomorrow and Audrey is riding her bicycle home, I can't really use "lack of room" as an excuse.

I try not to let this bug me. It's *good* that Blake has endeared himself to the other band members. Everybody should get along. There's nothing to be gained from three months of telling Blake that he can't ride with us and that we're going to check the drums for fingerprints when we get back, so the jerk should keep his filthy hands off them.

Still, I find myself weirdly disappointed when Blake doesn't make any condescending remarks about my automobile in front of Mel and Clarissa. I kind of want to egg him on ("So, Blake, what's your opinion on the suspension in this vehicle?") to find out if he's truly two-faced or if he really was tired and grumpy before. But everybody would see my true motives, and I'd be the bad guy.

I pull into Clarissa's driveway. "See you tomorrow," she tells Mel and me as she gets out of the car. "Nice to meet you, Blake."

Nice to meet you, Blake.

She might as well have said, "Will you be my boyfriend, you great, big, ol' hunk of man?" How can it possibly have been nice to meet Blake? Meeting Blake is the opposite of nice!

"Nice to meet you too," says Blake. That part I can get behind. I'm sure meeting Clarissa was very nice for him.

"Hopefully, I'll see you at school tomorrow," says Clarissa.

I'm sure she's being polite. It's not like they're gazing lovingly into each other's eyes or anything like that. She didn't ask if he wanted to hang out. She said she'd see him at school. Nothing wrong with that. My bandmates are not required to treat Blake with disdain.

"Yes, I'm looking forward to it," says Blake with a smile.

How dare he smile? He has no right to smile!

I remember a time when I could smile. Friday was a good day.

Clarissa closes the car door, and I pull out of her driveway. She doesn't turn back to blow Blake a kiss, and Blake isn't watching her with love in his eyes, so I don't need to freak out. They aren't going to get married and have a bunch of half-cool, half-devil kids.

I probably *should* root for them to get together because if they got into a fight, Clarissa could snap Blake in half over her knee like a twig. It would be fun to see Blake get snapped, but the mental scars of knowing that he was dating my drummer would never fade. I'd be ninety years old and having occasional screaming fits from thinking about them holding hands.

Anyway, as I have been about 372,218 times since Blake showed up in Florida, I'm being ridiculous. Clarissa is not going to go out with Blake. If he asked her, he'd get a drumstick through the nose.

A few minutes later, I pull into Mel's driveway. "Thanks for the ride," he tells me.

"No problem."

"Nice to meet you," he says to Blake. Clearly, he didn't notice my revulsion when Clarissa said those same words, or he wouldn't have spoken them.

"Nice to meet you too," says Blake.

They fist-bump.

Fist-bump!

Did you see that? No, no, of course you didn't. I'm the

one describing everything. But did you see the part where I said that they fist-bumped? I want to make sure you didn't skip over it. They fist-bumped! You can politely shake hands with somebody that you can't stand, but a fist bump implies that you tolerate a person, maybe even are *friends* with that person.

Oh, I left this out of the description because it was too painful, but you deserve to know. Mel initiated the fist bump.

It's as if their fists connect in slow motion, creating a friendship explosion. I haven't felt this betrayed since Clarissa told Blake it was nice to meet him. And for the record, Blake is terrible at fist-bumping. There's no technique. No style. He sort of makes a fist and moves his hand forward. I think he's worried that it might hurt.

Then Mel holds up his fist to me, and I'm so frazzled that for a split second that I think he's going to punch me. But then I accept the fist bump, even though I hate the idea of bumping a fist that bumped Blake's fist.

"Seeya," says Mel, getting out of the car.

Blake also gets out of the car and then gets into the front seat. Wow. He opened both doors himself. Is he showing off for Mel?

Blake puts on his seat belt. "Thanks for letting me come along."

"Sure."

"I like your bandmates."

I back out of Mel's driveway. "Good job fooling them."

Blake looks confused. "What do you mean?"

"You know what I mean."

"How did I fool them?"

"You know."

"Clearly, I don't, or I wouldn't be asking."

"I disagree. I think you would be asking if you knew, and I think that's what you're doing. You know, and you're asking. It's the kind of thing you do."

"Are you okay? Should you be driving?"

I pull away from Mel's house. "Admit it. You pretended to be decent."

"That's absurd."

"Do you mean you didn't pretend to be decent or that you weren't decent? Because you were decent. I'm saying it was an act instead of your natural self."

"You need to take a deep breath," says Blake.

He's right. I do.

He continues, "Breathe in, hold it for five seconds, and breathe out. Very slowly. Breathe in and breathe out. Close your eyes and...no, wait. Don't close your eyes. Eyes open at all times while driving. But breathe in..."

"I don't need you to talk me through it," I say, following his instructions. I breathe in, hold it for five seconds, and breathe out.

"Again," says Blake.

"I'll decide when I'm done breathing."

"Rod, I think you need to do something to manage your stress level, or you're going to have a heart attack at seventeen."

"What's your plan here?" I ask.

"You mean my nefarious scheme where I'm nice to your friends so they'll be my friends too?"

"Yes! That one!"

"They're going to be at our house all the time, right? Why shouldn't I hang out with them? It's not like I'm going to turn them against you or anything."

"You got your own lemonade. You opened the car door by yourself. You didn't make any subtle insults."

"And that's what you consider scheming?"

"From you, yes."

"Listen to yourself. If I were recording this conversation, which I'm not, and I played it back, I think you'd be surprised by how crazed you sound. Your mom would be worried about you. Who knows where that could lead?"

"Are you threatening to play this conversation for my mom?"

"No."

"See, that's the kind of thing you do! You create scenarios where you might have been recording me and float the possibility that I might get carted away to an asylum to make me paranoid! I'm sick of it."

"Stop sign," says Blake.

"What?"

"Stop sign."

"Is that the phrase you use to try to make people quit talking?"

"No, I was saying that there was a stop sign. You just drove through the intersection."

"Oh." That wasn't good. I don't want to get into a car crash, especially since the other vehicle might hit my side instead of Blake's. I take some more deep breaths.

"Whatever it is you think I'm doing, believe me, it's all in your mind. I don't want to live with you any more than you want me there, but there's nothing either of us can do about it, so we might as well try to get along. I'm not going to steal your girlfriend or your friends. I'll be gone in three months, and your life will be back to normal."

"I never thought you were going to steal Audrey," I tell him.

"Good. Because I'm not."

"It was never a possibility."

"I agree."

"She's not attracted to you."

"Nor I to her."

"Yeah, right."

"Not my type," says Blake.

"What is your type?"

"Taller."

"Like Clarissa?"

"Maybe."

"She'll never go out with you."

"I'm sure you're right."

"Seriously. It'll never happen."

"You'd know better than I would."

"So don't even think about it."

"There's no reason I shouldn't think about it," says Blake. "I think about lots of girls that would never talk to me. I also think about being Batman. You think about being Batman too, don't you?"

"Sometimes," I admit.

"So I'll think about dating Clarissa the same way I'd think about being Batman. Does that work for you?"

"Yeah, sure, I guess. Just know that you're not fooling anybody."

"Well, technically, if I *was* trying to fool somebody, I could argue that I'm fooling Audrey, Clarissa, Mel, and your mother. Good thing I'm not actually trying to fool anybody, huh?"

I take a long, deep breath and count to five.

I pay attention to all the traffic signs and lights for the rest of the way home despite an odd desire to floor the gas pedal and speed toward a moving train.

Mom isn't home yet when we get back, but she'll be home soon, so I start dinner. Under normal circumstances I'd step up my culinary efforts if there was a guest, but since I'm trying to expose Blake as a fraud who's only pretending that he doesn't totally suck, I'm going with macaroni and cheese.

Not the good stuff. Not the kind where you get a fancy packet of cheese sauce to squeeze onto the macaroni, and there will be no effort to elevate the flavor profile with bacon or truffles. This is the powder kind of mac and cheese. Not Kraft, but the generic stuff. I'm surprised that "Macaroni & Cheese" is spelled correctly on the box. This is a meal reserved for nights when Mom and I are both exhausted and don't care what we have.

I start to boil the water. I go through the cupboards and

purposely select the plate that has the most chips for Blake. I bet he's the kind of guy who'd worry about bacteria lurking in a chipped plate.

Mom gets home while the macaroni is cooking. "Thank you for starting dinner," she says, giving me a hug. "How was practice?"

"Pretty good. Blake offered plenty of useful feedback. Dinner will be ready in a few minutes."

An alarm goes off to let me know that the macaroni is done. What I mean is that a timer goes off to let me know that I've cooked the macaroni for several minutes longer than the instructions say. Nice and mushy. Yum.

You're supposed to add milk and butter when you mix in the cheesy powder, but water works as well as milk, right? And I'm sure Blake will appreciate the health benefits of not adding butter.

I happily stir the grossest macaroni and cheese I could possibly make without giving away that I made it gross on purpose. I'd love to add a few tufts of cat fur (we don't own a cat, but our neighbor does) and some of my own saliva, but that would be going too far. It has to look like I made a legitimate effort to provide a tasty meal.

I pour the concoction onto the plates and announce that dinner is served.

Blake picks up his fork (yes, his fork has a tiny bit of dried food I stuck to one of the tines) and gazes at his plate. I doubt he'd want to eat this even if it was prepared properly. Dinner is going to be pure agony for him. I love it.

"Looks scrumptious," says Blake.

I smile. "Doesn't it?"

He scoops up a bite and pops it into his mouth. As he chews, I can see that he thinks it's utterly disgusting. Will he dare to be rude enough to say something? I mean, your manners would have to be astonishingly poor to speak ill of a meal your generous host prepared for you.

Blake swallows with some effort. "Mmm," he says.

Of course, the downside to my plan is that I have to eat this too. I take a bite, and it's even worse than I thought. I choke it down without gagging. "I sure do love macaroni and cheese," I say.

"Me too," says Blake, taking another bite. A bead of sweat trickles down his forehead. "Yummy."

"Would you like some ketchup?" I ask, holding a bottle toward him. "It's kind of watery, but still good."

Mom takes a bite of her dinner, chews for a second, and then sets down her fork. "Rod!"

"What?"

"You completely overcooked this. You can't serve this to

a guest. And it tastes like you mixed the cheese packet with water instead of milk."

I can't believe it. I thought Mom would eat my cooking without complaint. I've made plenty of terrible meals on accident, so I never imagined that she'd embarrass me in front of my own cousin.

She stands up and collects all three plates. "I'm sorry, Blake," she says. "He usually makes it better than this."

"I thought it was perfectly fine," says Blake.

"You don't have to be polite in this household," Mom informs him. "That was inedible. C'mon, Rod, you know better than that."

It would appear that my plan has backfired.

"Sorry," I say. "I never claimed to be a master chef."

"It's macaroni and cheese. An eight-year-old can make macaroni and cheese."

"I don't know about that," says Blake. "I was involved in lots of macaroni and cheese–related mishaps when I was a preteen. One time for St. Patrick's Day I added green food coloring, and I got it all over my shirt. Food coloring doesn't come out of clothing very well, and my mom was hopping mad. So don't give Rod too hard of a time over this."

"Well, Rod isn't eight."

"Fair enough," says Blake. He looks at me. "I tried."

My face burns with anger and shame. All I wanted was for Blake to go "*Bleaarrrgh!*" and spit it back onto the plate. Was that so much to ask?

"Now what are we supposed to eat?" Mom asks.

Blake shrugs. "Pizza encore?"

"No, no, we're not doing pizza again. I'll make something else."

"What about Chinese? My treat."

"You're not buying us dinner again. Chinese sounds great, but you're not paying for it."

"I insist."

"Absolutely not."

The task of ordering and picking up dinner falls on me, though Mom doesn't go so far as to make me pay for it with my own money. I do a lot of deep breathing during the drive. A *lot* of deep breathing.

12.

I STARE AT my bedroom wall.

I can't be certain, but I think Blake moved all his posters about an inch onto my side. It's not enough that I can prove he did anything, though the subliminal impact is there. As soon as I stepped into my room, I thought, *He messed with the posters again.*

I'm not sure when he would have done it. It would've taken a while to move every single poster, and I don't think he's been in my room unattended tonight. He'd be taking a huge risk of getting caught. Still, I'm almost positive that his posters take up one more inch wall space than mine.

This must be part of his plan to make me doubt my sanity.

I should draw a line on the wall in case he does it again.

No, that's something that somebody who doubts their sanity would do.

I'll just be on high alert for the sound of pushpins being

pulled out of the Sheetrock and stuck back in again. I'm not saying that Blake won't drive me insane, but if he does, it won't be with my posters.

Actually, if he *did* move all his posters, there'll be separate holes in the wall one inch from where the corners of each poster are now. I walk over to the center of the wall and pull out the pin in the upper left corner of a poster featuring a raccoon and the caption "Stick 'Em Up!" (Presumably, the raccoon looks like a bank robber wearing a mask. This doesn't seem to be a clever enough visual for somebody to translate into poster form, but I won't judge.)

There isn't an extra hole in the wall one inch away.

I check the lower left corner to be sure.

Nope. No extra hole. In fact, it looks like Blake considerately used the same holes from the posters of mine that he took down.

Fine. Maybe he's not performing slight rearrangements of our decor in an attempt to make me question my sense of reality. That doesn't mean he's not a jerk.

"What are you doing?" a voice asks behind me.

(Spoiler alert: The voice belongs to Blake. You probably guessed that, but if even one of you reading this said, "Wow, I bet there's a major plot twist about to be revealed regarding the identity of the person who asked what he was doing!" then I'll consider my attempt to draw out the suspense a success.)

I turn around. "Oh, hi, Blake."

"Why are you messing with my poster?"

"I'm not," I say, quickly squeezing my hand closed, which isn't something I recommend when you're holding a pushpin. Fortunately, I'm composed enough not to wince in pain as the pin jabs through my tender flesh.

"Yes, you are. It's flopping over."

"Don't tell me what to do in my own room."

"I wasn't," says Blake. "I was asking a question. You got all bent out of shape when I touched your posters, so I assumed that you'd respect mine. I already offered to take them down."

"Sorry," I say. "I walked in here, and there was movement behind the raccoon poster. I thought there might be a centipede behind it or something. I figured you didn't want a big bug slithering back there, so I took out two of the pins so I could check to be sure. Turns out there's no centipede. Good to hear, right? Centipede juice doesn't come out of posters well."

"Centipede juice?"

I nod. "It's what you get when you squish a centipede. I thought that if you saw your poster moving, you might slap it. So I did you a favor."

"I'm pretty sure you didn't."

"Well, like I said, there wasn't anything back there, so I guess it was a hallucination on my part. That happens sometimes." I stick one of the pins back in the corner of the poster.

"Was there blood on that pin?"

"Nope."

"Is there blood on your palm?"

"Nope."

"I think there is."

"I think maybe you should worry about your own palms." I replace the second pin. "Whammo. Good as new."

"Did you say whammo?"

"Yes. And I'll say it again."

Blake is quiet for a moment. "Well, let me know if you have any other centipede sightings. Working as a team, I'm sure we can defeat the centipede menace."

Blake leaves my bedroom.

I wonder if he did that trick where you smear toothpaste on the wall to fill in the holes made by pushpins.

I decide not to check.

I drive to school every morning. I assume I'll have to tell Blake, "Sorry, dude. Looks like you're taking the bus," but

Mom has to sign some paperwork at the school, so she's driving him today.

Fortunately, we'll only share two classes—third-period English and seventh-period biology. Oh, and lunch. I hope he'll make some friends before lunch so he won't want to sit with me.

For my first two classes, it's a completely normal day. I can't remember if I said this before, but I'm a pretty good student. I pay attention in class, and when Mr. Gellbar springs a pop quiz on us, I'm confident that I got at least a nine out of ten.

When I sit down in English class, I'm glad that my assigned seat is in the middle of the room with classmates to my front, rear, left, and right. The one vacant seat is in the back. Blake won't be sitting next to me.

Blake walks in as the bell rings. I was sort of hoping that he'd get hopelessly lost in the labyrinth, but I guess somebody gave him directions.

Ms. Mayson, who looks like she's about eighty, but also looks like she could, if necessary, beat up the entire class like she was in a kung fu movie, walks to the front of the room with Blake. "As you know, we have a new student today. He'll be joining us while his mom and dad are doing missionary work in Ecuador. Please welcome Blake Montgomery."

It's not clear if we're supposed to applaud or say, "Hello, Blake Montgomery," or what, so everybody just kind of sits there.

"Why don't you tell the class a little about yourself, Blake?" asks Ms. Mayson.

I can't help but sympathize with him. No student in the history of the school system has ever wanted to stand up in front of a class and tell everyone a little about themselves.

"I'm Rodney's cousin," he begins.

Ugh. Everybody already knew that my cousin was joining our class, but I still don't like hearing him say it out loud.

"Usually, when my parents are off doing diplomatic work, they go separately, or if it's during the summer, I go with them. This time it was too good of an opportunity to help the Ecuadorian people to pass up, so I'm staying with Rodney and my aunt. I guess my parents were worried that a party animal like me would trash the house while they were gone."

The class chuckles. I wonder why he won't admit that his parents are on a cruise. Or did I miss some important detail of my mom's story?

"What are your hobbies?" asks Ms. Mayson.

"Oh, a little of this, a little of that," says Blake. "I dabble in filmmaking, writing, painting, mentoring. Jack of all trades, master of none, right?"

"I hear that," says Ms. Mayson, even though she's been an English teacher for decades.

"I had to leave my motorcycle behind in California, which was a major disappointment. My daily ride gets rid of a lot of stress. I'm not trying to brag. I don't do tricks or anything. Just me on the open road, seventy miles per hour, wind racing through my hair. I miss that."

I raise my hand. "You don't wear a helmet?"

Ms. Mayson shushes me.

"I should. I really should," says Blake. "My craving for danger is going to get me in trouble someday."

I glance around the classroom. Nobody is actually buying this, are they? I mean, c'mon. Everybody should be rolling their eyes. They should be pointing and laughing, not in a mean-spirited bullying way, just showing Blake they know he's making up all this stuff about craving danger. The only danger he craves is eating a microwave burrito before it's cooled down.

But my classmates seem to be buying his story.

"My newest endeavor is music," Blake tells the class.

"Oh?" asks Ms. Mayson. "Which instrument do you play?"

"None. I only wish I were that talented. But I'm an advisor to my cousin Rodney's band, Fanged Grapefruit."

I'll let the diplomatic mission and the fake hobbies and the motorcycle stuff slide, but no way is Blake going to stand up in front of the class and say that he's an advisor to Fanged Grapefruit.

"No, you're not," I protest.

"Didn't I provide feedback after your last rehearsal?"

"That doesn't make you an advisor."

"Wasn't the feedback incorporated into the end product?"

"You're not an advisor."

"Don't argue with your cousin on his first day," Ms. Mayson tells me. "That's very juvenile."

"I'm setting the record straight."

"Record," says Blake. "That's an appropriate pun for a band."

The class chuckles.

"Anyway," says Blake. "I hope you'll all come to the Lane tonight to see the new and improved Fanged Grapefruit. It'll be a great show."

"Thank you, Blake," says Ms. Mayson. She points to the empty seat in the back. "You can sit there for now."

Blake smiles and takes his seat.

He's not our advisor! I start counting to five again.

We're reading this book called *Falling Leaves of the Life Tree*, which is not the real name of the book, but even though the author has been dead for about a hundred and fifty years, I don't want to name the actual book in case the author's descendants are sensitive and litigious.

Ms. Mayson has us read chapter twelve silently for about ten minutes.

"Ye who catch not the leaves see not the tree," spoke Count Vargas. "If you gaze forth, why not gaze about instead?"

Guntheramous gave a nod of his weighty head. "Yours wisd'm haith giv'n this olde head a scritcher to puzzle, mightn't it? Would ye confiss ta stailin' such mind-thoughts from ye ailders?"

"Speaketh not that blasphemy lest thy cleft of chin meet the steel tip of my dagger," Count Vargas gasped in rage.

"I'm an advisor for Fanged Grapefruit," Blake Montgomery told the Count.

"Liar! Fraudulent liar!" shouted Count Vargas, waving his dagger to and fro. "Thou shalt suffer dearly for this falsehood! Guntheramous! Slay him thusly!"

"But Count Vargas of Wicktensteinberg, my faingers, when clutched, containen naught to call a weapoun!"

"Then slay him with thy bare hands! Tear his head from his shoulders, then his arms from their sockets, then his fingers from their finger sockets, then his legs from his torso, and then squeeze his torso until all contents doth spill forth, and then tread firmly upon them!"

"Uh-oh," said Blake Montgomery. "I'm in a heap o' trouble now!"

And Guntheramous, he did attack, and he did tear the rascal limb from limb. As Blake Montgomery spilled, he cursed the wretched day that he deceptively told a classroom of students that he was in any way associated with such a fine group of musicians as Fanged Grapefruit. His eyes closed, everything went dark, but it didn't go dark because his eyes were closed (sorry to confuse ye) but rather because he was dead.

Should I be worried that I'm inserting Blake's demise into scenes of classic literature that I'm reading for English class? Probably, but I'll worry about it later. And just hope there isn't a pop quiz before then.

unlucky

13. (A.K.A. "THE GROSS CHAPTER")
(WARNING: DO NOT READ.)

FOURTH PERIOD IS much better because Blake isn't there. Then it's lunchtime, where I sit with Audrey and Mel every day. (Clarissa has second lunch. Luckily, she has many other friends besides us, so she's has people to eat with. She's fine.)

To actually refuse to let Blake sit with us would feel like bullying, so I work out a two-part strategy:

1. Hope that Blake doesn't sit at my table.
2. If he does, try to avoid knocking myself unconscious from repeatedly bashing my head against the table in frustration.

It turns out that I don't even see Blake. Maybe he's eating outside. Maybe he'll eat outside every day for the next three months, and it'll be one less problem for me to deal with. Knowing Blake, he's probably having sushi delivered.

Mel and Audrey, perhaps noticing a twitch in my

eyebrow, do not mention Blake the entire time. It's half an hour of happiness.

Fifth period is fine. Sixth period, physical education, is also fine because running while a gym teacher yells at me to run faster is a hobby of mine. (I'm actually a good runner. All the jumping around I do while playing music keeps me in good shape.)

Seventh period, as you may or may not recall, is biology. I've always enjoyed this class. Not enough to become a doctor or marine biologist, but enough to look forward to the labs and stuff. Audrey is my lab partner, but even if my lab partner was Stinky Frank, the Deodorant-Free Kid, I'd enjoy it.

But today, there's a new student in seventh-period biology, one I want to be farther away from than Stinky Frank. And that student is…you know.

(Fun fact: One day Stinky Frank came into school wearing an automobile air freshener around his neck. He has a good sense of humor about his aromatic challenges. I think it gives him a sense of identity and purpose. He's very odd but always kind.)

Mr. Gy doesn't make Blake stand in front of the class and tell them a little about himself. "Gretchen is out today, but she'll be your lab partner in the future," Mr. Gy tells him. "For now, your cousin can show you the ropes."

Blake walks over to my and Audrey's station. Today we're doing dissections.

I quickly hold my notebook over the specimen, as it occurs to me that this might be really upsetting for him. (Blake, not the specimen, although I suppose things aren't going so great for the specimen either.) It's probably the last thing he wants to dissect.

"Maybe you should join one of the other tables," I say. "Julie and Mark are dissecting a squid."

"What are you dissecting?" Blake asks.

"You don't want to know."

"What is it?" he presses.

"A rat."

"Oh, cool!"

"I thought you loved rats."

"I do. That doesn't mean I don't want to dissect one."

I move my notebook. The dead rat is on its back in a tray. If you read the warning at the beginning of this chapter and assumed I was talking about snot or something, you have my permission to skip to the next chapter. We are, indeed, going to cut this rat open. It's for science.

"Awesome," Blake says with way too much enthusiasm. "Can we get started, or are there instructions?"

"There are instructions," says Audrey.

Blake looks disappointed.

Next to the tray is a piece of paper with a drawing of a rat showing where to make the incisions and written step-by-step instructions about how to cut up the rat and what we're supposed to learn while we're doing it. We have a tiny pair of scissors, which we will use to make an incision in the abdominal wall.

"What should we name it?" asks Blake.

"Nothing," I say.

"How about Reginald the Rat? Ronald the Rat? Roberto the Rat? It doesn't matter to me as long as it starts with an R."

"We don't name specimens before we dissect them," says Audrey. "That's cruel."

"Why is it cruel?"

"Because then you think about how the rat used to be alive."

"Not me," says Blake. "When I think of Roberto the Rat, I think of a cartoon character."

"I thought you hated cartoons," I say.

"I do. That's why it doesn't bug me to dissect Roberto the Rat."

I pick up the scissors. "I'll be making the incision."

"Why?"

"Because you'll cackle while you do it."

"I will not cackle," he insists.

"Fine. You'll giggle."

"I can't believe that we have the same grandparents and yet you think I'd cackle and giggle while I slice up a rat."

"I can't believe we're related either, but here we are."

"Is everything all right?" asks Mr. Gy from across the room.

"Yes, sir," I say. "Just working out our plan of attack."

"Follow the instructions on the paper."

"We will."

I touch the scissors to Roberto's tummy, and then I [*description deleted*]. After that, I [*worse description deleted*], making sure not to damage the underlying structures. Then I open the flaps.

"Now it says to rinse out the body cavity," says Blake. "Can I give him the shower?"

I shake my head. "You're an observer for today."

The three of us being lab partners today is actually working out really well. Blake is no longer the charming guy who offers constructive criticism on a musical performance. He's the creepy guy who wants to leer at rat guts. Audrey is finally seeing the true Blake.

Audrey picks up the tray. "I'll rinse it out," she says, walking over to the sink.

"You're a lucky man," says Blake. "I don't know many girls who would volunteer to rinse out a dead rat's body cavity."

"We're in biology class."

"Still…"

Moments later Audrey returns with the freshly rinsed rat. Now our task is to look at various organs and glands and correctly identify them. Some are easy. (Everybody knows what lungs look like.) And some are difficult. (Do *you* know where the thymus gland is?) When we think we've got it right, we're supposed to alert Mr. Gy, who will observe as we point to and name each blob of rat gunk.

He walks over, and Audrey and I trade off identifying the parts in the first layer. "Excellent," says Mr. Gy. "Now remove the peritoneum."

"What's the peritoneum?" Blake asks.

I look down at the sheet. "A membrane."

"Nice."

You don't want to read about me removing a membrane (or *do* you?) (weirdo), especially because I don't get it completely right the first time. But soon we have a whole new layer of organs for our identifying pleasure. These are grosser than the ones on top. No matter what the creature, a stomach isn't an organ you want to look at for very long.

We identify them among ourselves, and then call Mr. Gy

over. We don't get them all right (curse you, esophagus!), but we do well enough that the rat's feelings wouldn't be hurt.

"Good job," says Mr. Gy. "There's going to be a quiz, so keep practicing until all three of you are comfortable identifying everything."

Mr. Gy walks over to watch the kids who are dissecting an alligator. (I'm kidding. It's a frog. Just making sure you're paying attention.)

"Do you know all the parts?" I ask Blake.

He nods. "The caudate lobe is my favorite."

"Of course it is."

"I hope this rat doesn't come back to life and seek vengeance," he adds.

With anybody else, I'd be thrilled to chat about zombie rats, but I don't want to squander that subject on Blake. I ignore his comment and focus my attention on the guts.

"Do you need the tools anymore?" Audrey asks. "If you don't, I'll wash them off."

"I wouldn't mind poking around in there a little more," says Blake.

"I'll wash them off now," says Audrey.

Even if my girlfriend doesn't know that Blake is pure evil, she now knows that he's uncool.

Audrey goes over to the sink. Her back is to us, which

means that she doesn't see Blake poke his gloved index finger into the rat.

"Knock it off," I whisper.

"What's the matter?" he whispers back. "Worried about maintaining an antiseptic environment for our patient? I don't think Roberto has to worry about infection."

I don't answer him. I shouldn't have to explain why it's not okay to stick your finger into a dissected rat.

Blake glances around the classroom. Nobody is paying attention.

He reaches into the rat and scoops up some…uh, *contents*. *Please don't eat it*, I think. *Please, please, please don't eat it.*

He doesn't eat it. Even Blake has higher standards than that.

He holds up his hand and looks into my eyes.

If he throws that at me, he'll regret it until his dying day, which will be today. If he throws it at me, I'll make sure that he's expelled and that Aunt Mary and Uncle Clark have to cut their stupid cruise short to come get him. There is no decision he can make in life that's worse than throwing rat innards at me.

He doesn't throw it at me.

He throws them at himself.

Roberto's insides strike Blake directly in the forehead. He recoils and cries out in disgust. "Ew! Rod, *dude*!"

Everybody in the class turns to look.

Blake frantically wipes his face with the back of his hand. "Ew, ew, ew! What's the matter with you?"

"Are you out of your mind?" asks Mr. Gy, striding toward me with the look of a teacher who assumed that he could trust us to do dissections without starting a food fight.

"I didn't do it!" I insist. "He did it to himself!"

"I get that you're cousins and used to horsing around with each other, but this is completely unacceptable. Get him a wet towel!"

"He threw it in his own face!" I say.

I look over at Audrey, who is staring at me with her mouth wide open.

"I said to get him a wet towel," Mr. Gy tells me. I've never seen a teacher look so angry.

"So gross…so gross," says Blake. "It got on the floor too. I'll get the towel."

He steps forward, pretends to slip on something slimy, and falls to the floor as everybody in the biology lab gasps. I'll give him credit for being committed to the role. That fall looks like it hurt.

I've never been afraid of a challenge, but trying to convince everybody that Blake threw the rat guts in his own face is not going to be easy. Blake definitely wins this round.

14.

RECAP FOR THOSE *who skipped chapter thirteen due to the grossness factor*: Our hero, Rod, was in biology class, where he was lab partners with his amazing girlfriend, Audrey, and his rotten cousin, Blake. After successfully dissecting a rat and identifying its parts, Audrey stepped away from the table, at which point Blake threw some rat bits into his own face, but he pretended that Rod did it! That's right. He framed Rod! What's up with that?

Official apology for those who skipped chapter thirteen due to the grossness factor and then still had to read about rat guts in the recap: Sorry.

Blake and I sit in Principal Gordon's office. Principal Gordon is a medium-sized man with a small head and large arms. He's a friendly guy when he's addressing the school at assemblies or when you pass him in the hallway, but he doesn't like troublemakers. I know students who've found themselves in my current position, and they've spun tales of a man who made them feel like he would devote every waking moment for the rest of his long, long life to making them pay for their transgressions. They'd be forty years old with a spouse, children, a beautiful home, a lucrative and personally satisfying job, and think to themselves, *Yep, everything sure worked out.* Moments later Principal Gordon would step out from behind a tree and reveal that this was all part of his elaborate plan for vengeance. The spouse, the kids, the home, the job—all of them had been set up by Principal Gordon, and he was taking them away, leaving the misbehaving student alone, homeless, jobless, and weeping softly as storm clouds formed in the dark sky.

This always seemed far-fetched. Still, it successfully conveyed the message that it was better not to find yourself in the principal's office.

"Mr. Conklin," he says with the frown of a person who could destroy a student's future. "I haven't seen you in my office before."

"No, sir," I say. My school record is flawless. I save the antics for the stage.

"Let me make sure I understand what happened. You were in lab, learning about the interior of a rodent, and you flung viscera into Mr. Montgomery's face?"

I shake my head. "He threw it into his own face."

"Why would he throw it into his own face?"

"To make you think I threw it into his face."

Principal Gordon turns to Blake. "Mr. Montgomery, is that true?"

"No, sir."

Principal Gordon turns back to me. "He says he didn't do it."

"He's lying."

"Calling somebody a liar is a strong accusation, Mr. Conklin. You have to understand that when I'm reviewing two very different accounts of what happened, I'm more inclined to believe the one where a student *didn't* throw rat guts in his own face."

"I understand," I say. "But that's what happened."

"Why would he do that? You couldn't pay me enough to do that to myself. Mr. Montgomery, did you *enjoy* what happened?"

"No, sir," says Blake. "The experience will haunt me."

"I have to go with the story that sounds the most credible. I've had some strange, strange kids in my office over the years. I once had a kid who ate an entire tub of paste. Obviously, this was when I was an elementary school principal; students tend to grow out of the paste-eating phase by the time they're teenagers. But he ate an entire tub. I don't mean a small tub either. We had to call an ambulance. You'd think there'd be a point when he'd say to himself, 'Okay, I've eaten enough paste for one sitting.' But no. He gorged himself. And it was *not* easy for the doctors to get all that paste out of him. And that kid *still* doesn't compare to somebody smearing a dissected rat in his own face."

"It wasn't smeared," I say. "It was thrown."

"By you?"

"No."

"By who then?"

"Blake! By Blake!"

"Are you sure you're not protecting another student?"

"Principal Gordon, I know it sounds deranged, but I'm telling the truth."

"You two are cousins, right?"

"Yes."

"That explains it," the principal says, looking satisfied.

"How does that explain anything?" I ask.

"Cousins are known for their hijinks. This one got out of hand." Principal Gordon clears his throat. "Mr. Montgomery, this was a terrible way for you to be welcomed to our school, and I regret that your educational experience has been clouded by the event. Since there were no witnesses and there's a difference in opinion about what actually happened, I'm not going to punish anybody, but Mr. Conklin, I'm going to ask you to apologize."

"He doesn't have to apologize," says Blake. "He may have thrown them on accident."

"He shouldn't have been holding rat parts in the first place. I know proper dissection protocol. Mr. Gy would never have you mucking around in there."

"My hands are clean," I protest.

"Enough," says Principal Gordon. "We're done with the debate. Apologize to your cousin, and I'll send you on your way."

"I'm sorry, Rodney," says Blake.

"Not you."

"Oh, my mistake. I have guilt issues, so I apologize a lot even when it's supposed to be somebody apologizing to me."

"Mr. Conklin?"

I consider refusing to back down, but what will that get me? They'll call Mom. I might get suspended, and this whole situation will turn into even more of a mess than it already is. Even I'm having trouble believing what Blake did, so how am I going to convince anybody else?

I look at Blake. "I'm sorry for what happened," I say. I figure that counts as a real apology, but is vague enough that I'm not admitting guilt.

"Do you accept your cousin's apology, Mr. Montgomery?"

"Yes, of course I do. We're family."

"Good. There's clearly some tension between you two, and you need to work it out before this escalates. I don't expect to see either of you in my office again. You're dismissed."

"How'd it go?" asks Audrey, walking up to my locker.

"He let us off with a warning." I spin the dial again. I'm so stressed out right now that I can't get my combination right.

"That's good."

"Yeah."

"Why'd you do it?"

I stare at her. "What?"

"Why'd you do that? You knew you'd get in trouble. Why are you putting your future at risk?"

"I didn't do anything!"

"It doesn't seem like something anybody would do to themselves. I can't imagine wanting to get somebody in trouble so much that I'd splat a rat into my face."

"Well, you're not Blake. C'mon, Audrey, you can't really believe that I did it. You're supposed to be on my side."

"You were pretty mad at him."

"So?"

"So, maybe you lost your temper…"

"No! He set me up! He knew nobody would believe that he'd do something so gross, and he was right! Even my own girlfriend doesn't believe me!"

"I'm not saying I don't believe you."

"You just did."

Audrey furrows her brow in concentration as if giving careful consideration to what she's about to say. This can't be good.

"All I'm saying is that you've been frustrated with him since he got here and I want you to think before you act. That's all."

"I can't believe you're on Team Blake!"

"I'm not on Team Blake," Audrey insists. "I don't even like him all that much. I just think that your resentment is coming out in unhealthy ways."

"You know what? Fine." I still can't get my locker open. I yank on the lock, hard, hoping that the adrenaline flowing through my body is so intense that I can tear off the lock and impress Audrey with my Hulk strength. But the adrenaline lets me down, and I may have pulled a muscle in my arm.

"What would Blake hope to accomplish?" Audrey asks.

"This! What's happening right now is what he hopes to accomplish!"

"But why?"

"I don't know. Jealousy? Thirst for power? Attention? I don't *want* to understand Blake's mind. It's dark and scary. Are you breaking up with me?"

"No! I'm just asking you to be nice to him. It was hard enough to get my mom to let me date a punk rocker. She won't let me date a delinquent."

"All right," I say. "I promise that I will never again do the thing I didn't do."

"Thank you."

"You're welcome."

"Do you need help with your locker?"

"No. I'll get it eventually."

Audrey pats me on the arm, which is as close as she'll ever get to a public display of affection, and then walks away. I finally get my combination right and take off the lock.

"Dude!" says Craig "the Craigster" Jones. "I can't believe you threw a squid in his face! That was awesome!"

"We were dissecting a rat."

"I can't believe you threw the rat in his face! That was awesome!"

"Thanks."

Blake is waiting next to my car when I walk through the student parking lot. Stuffing him into the trunk will only make my problems worse, so I unlock the door. We get in.

"How was your day?" he asks as I start the engine.

"It was quite bad."

"Sorry to hear it. This is a decent enough school. The building itself could use a little more upkeep. But the kids are nice, and the teachers seem educated."

I say nothing as I pull out of the parking lot and onto the street.

"Sorry about our misunderstanding in biology class," says Blake.

"How was that in any way a misunderstanding?"

"Because I don't understand why you did it."

"Did what?"

"You know what you did. I think there's still a piece of sinew between my teeth."

"First of all, sinew comes from tendons or ligaments. You didn't get hit in the face with any sinew, and if you did, you didn't get hit with it at a high enough velocity for it to get stuck between your teeth. So your story is falling apart."

"I'm not good at biology. Also, I had a candy bar later, so

it could be nougat. Doesn't taste like nougat, but what does nougat even taste like?"

I'm infuriated all over again. And I want answers. "Why'd you do it?"

"Because I was startled. Trust me—I didn't want to get you in trouble. But when something like that happens, I don't care how dignified you are, you're going to yelp."

"I didn't throw anything at you."

"Then who did?"

"You did!"

"Doesn't sound like something I would do."

"Are you kidding me? Are you really sticking to your ridiculous story even though we're the only two people in the car?"

"I'm a warrior for the truth," says Blake.

"Okay, I get what's happening." I dig out my cell phone and hand it to him. "I'm not recording this. You can confirm it. You won't be incriminating yourself, so you can drop the act."

He hands me my cell phone without looking at it. "There's no act. You treated me less like a cousin and more like a clown at a dunk tank. I trusted you to make my first day at a new school a comfortable experience, and instead you humiliated me in front of everybody. You know what they call me now? Rat Gut Face. Even Mr. Gy calls me that."

"Mr. Gy does *not* call you Rat Gut Face."

"He thinks it."

"Nobody calls you that. And if they did, it's actually kind of a cool nickname, but they don't, so it doesn't matter. I don't know why you're trying to ruin my life, but I'd appreciate it if you'd stop."

"You can lie to me, Rod, but you can't lie to yourself. When you look into the mirror, you'll know who did it."

"Yes, I'll see you standing behind me in the mirror because you're hogging half of my room!"

"Is that why you attacked me? You're still upset about your room? I can sleep out in the shed if that's what you want."

"We don't have a shed."

"Should we build one together? It could be a bonding experience."

"Look," I say, "I don't know what kind of demented game you're playing, but it needs to stop. I'm on to you, and you won't get away with this kind of stuff again. I'd advise you to go to school, study hard, keep your head down, and stop trying to ruin my life."

"Why would I want to ruin your life, Rod?"

"I don't know."

"If you don't know, perhaps it's because there's no reason."

"Maybe you're a deeply miserable person. Maybe you hate your life in California. Maybe you can't stand to see me being happy."

"You're poor. Your dad left you. Your band hasn't had any real success. Your friends only use you for your garage. What do have you to be happy about?"

I'll be honest. If there was a tray of rat innards on the dashboard, I'd fling it at him.

"Being poor has nothing to do with my happiness," I say. "Some of us don't need to pay people to cater to our every whim. Don't talk about my dad. I don't expect my band to be a superstar success because we're in *high school*. And my friends do *not* use me for my garage."

"That's what they want you to think."

"I don't even have the best garage."

"Then why do you practice there?"

"Because my mom usually isn't home."

"So they only use you for your mom's absence."

"Your mind games aren't going to work on me. You've picked the wrong opponent," I inform him. "I may seem lovable, but I will *destroy* you if you don't back off."

"Why are you so hostile? I accepted your apology."

"I mean it, Blake. You think you're some master manipulator, but you're wrong. This is over."

"If I *was* trying to manipulate you, which I'm not, I'm just getting started."

"I've given you your final warning. Knock it off. We're done talking."

"All right," says Blake. "I think this was a very illuminating conversation."

"Whatever."

"I'm looking forward to seeing your band tonight," he says.

"No, you can't come."

"I want to see how the audience responds to the way I revamped your sound."

"You didn't revamp anything. All you did was...no, I'm done. I don't expect to see you anywhere near the Lane tonight. If I find you within a *mile* of the club, we're going to have a problem."

"Is your house within a mile of the club?"

"No."

"Okay. I'll stay home then."

15.

I'M NOT GOING to let Cousin Blake ruin my life.

I'm not going to let Cousin Blake ruin my life.

I'm not going to let Cousin Blake ruin my life.

I'm not going to let Cousin Blake ruin my life.

I'm not going to let Cousin Blake ruin my life.

I'm not going to repeat things in my mind over and over and over until I feel like I'm going crazy.

He's made a terrible mistake. I'm a well-liked guy. Maybe people will take his side at the beginning, but in the long term, Team Blake is going to have exactly one member. (Blake.)

Fanged Grapefruit is setting up at the Lane. *Trivia*: experts have counted twenty-three different types of stains on the ceiling, only six of which they've been able to successfully identify. I feel good about tonight's show. The headliner is a group from Atlanta called Bathtub Scum, and they're so popular that I think as many as a dozen people could show up early enough to see our act.

We don't say much as we set up. Mel and Clarissa both know what happened in biology class, but I guess they don't want to bring it up in case it messes with my mojo before the show. Everybody in the band is very respectful of one another's mojo.

Audrey, as always, is working the merch table. She smiles as I look over at her. Ha! Try as he might, Blake wasn't able to get my girlfriend to stop smiling at me!

By eight o'clock, I'm disappointed that there are only seven other people in the club. Bathtub Scum has a reputation for showing up to their gigs an hour late, smelling of gummy worms, so maybe their fans know not to get there too early. Oh well. We'll rock the house for these seven.

"Thanks for coming out tonight!" I say into the microphone. "Are you ready to *rock*?"

"Affirmative!" shouts the one guy who's actually looking at the stage.

"We're Grapefruit Fangs," I say. "And this first song is called…"

Grapefruit Fangs? Wait. What?

"I mean Fanged Grapefruit," I say, even though Grapefruit Fangs is kind of a cool name for a band too. "And this first song is an original called…"

Blake.

No, the first song isn't called "Blake." I mean that Blake walks into the Lane.

He's wearing jeans and a blue T-shirt. To better fit in with the punk rock crowd, he seems to have cut holes in his clothing. Despite this, he couldn't look more out of place if he were dressed for a rodeo.

He looks at me and gives me a thumbs-up.

I think Blake is counting on me being too professional to scream at him from the stage. And the little creep is right. I'm going to carry on as if he weren't there.

"This first song is an original called…"

Which song is first? What *are* our songs?

There is, of course, a set list taped to the floor next to my feet. "This first song is an original called…"

The one guy who was ready to rock looks like his readiness to rock is fading.

We were supposed to open with "The Night I Drank Way Too Many Blue Raspberry Slushes," but I don't think I can handle Blake's smug look if it goes well. I want to start with a song that he didn't influence. "Let's change things up," I say, turning around to look at Clarissa. "Let's do 'That Bandage Won't Keep Your Legs Attached.'"

"We haven't practiced that in months."

"It'll be okay." I turn back toward the tiny audience.

"This first song is an original called 'That Bandage Won't Keep Your Legs Attached.' *One, two, three, go!*"

Clarissa launches into the opening drum sequence. Mel joins in with lead guitar. I do my famous screech and then begin to sing.

The guy in the audience bounces around, body slamming invisible people.

Who cares if Blake is here? When I'm onstage, there's nothing he can do, except cause me to change my set list without informing my fellow band members and fluster me into forgetting the name of the first song. He's not going to bring me down. This is my world.

We're on fire tonight. Sure, there's only one guy bobbing his head to the beat, but his head is bobbing in a big way. By the third verse, I've almost forgotten that Blake exists.

The song ends, and the guy up front applauds with great enthusiasm. Blake (that kid I almost forgot about) applauds as well. Though he shouldn't be here at all, at least he's considerate enough to stay in the back. Or he's scared of being injured in the one-man mosh pit. Either way, I'm glad he's not near the stage.

We go into our second song, which was supposed to be the first song. I don't care if this song is .009 percent better because of Blake's input. Tonight is about the music and nothing else.

A tall skinny guy who's maybe a few years older than me walks into the club. He's wearing a black Fanged Grapefruit shirt. If this were a cartoon, which it might as well be, my eyes would pop out of their sockets on springs. I've never seen anybody in our band's T-shirt who wasn't (A) Mel, (B) Clarissa, (C) Audrey, (D) my mom, or (E) me.

It can't be a coincidence that he's wearing a Fanged Grapefruit shirt to a Fanged Grapefruit show. He must be a Fanged Grapefruit fan. A fan! An actual fan!

He walks up to the stage and begins to move to the music.

Two more people, a guy and a girl, walk into the Lane. They aren't wearing our band's T-shirts, but that's okay because they hurry up front. For those keeping track, we now have four people enjoying our music enough to move to the rhythm.

By the end of "The Night I Drank Way Too Many Blue Raspberry Slushes," there are six. One of them is a girl I sort of recognize from school. The rest look like college students.

"Thank you, everybody," I say as the song ends. "How many of you like chess?"

The crowd gives a huge cheer for the game of chess.

"Well, this song was inspired by that amazing feeling you get when you put your opponent into checkmate. It's called 'Checkmate, Checkmate, Checkmate,' and it goes like this!"

By the time *that* song is done, the size of our audience has doubled. One guy is wearing a Fanged Grapefruit sticker on his forehead. And I know you won't believe me, but there's a woman in the audience in one of our shirts. I knew that someday I'd see two Fanged Grapefruit shirts on two separate audience members at the same show, but I never imagined it would be tonight.

Did I mention that we're on fire? We're playing the best we've ever have. We're usually pretty good about covering wrong notes, but tonight there are no wrong notes to cover. More people come into the club with each song. I wonder if some of them happened to be walking by and said, "Wow, that band currently playing in the Lane sounds fantastic! It would be silly to keep walking past the club, which would take me out of earshot of that delightful music. I think I'll stroll inside and enjoy the rest of their set."

By the time we're on our last song, there are fifty people in the audience. That wasn't a typo. Fifty. Five-zero. Ten times five. Half of triple digits. Sure, if Adele walked out onstage and there were only fifty people, she might go ballistic and start firing her staff, but for us, this attendance is astounding. Fifty people! Listening to our music! Voluntarily!

I assume they're here voluntarily. None of them appear to be in handcuffs.

Not only have we never had a better show, but I'll go

so far as to say that I've never had a better half hour. Not during my fifth birthday party when Mom and Dad discovered the invitations had the wrong date so I got to eat all the cake myself. (They didn't give me permission to do this, but I didn't get in trouble for it since it was my birthday.) Not when I kicked the winning goal in a soccer game and the rest of the team carried me off the field in victory. (They accidentally dropped me, and I broke a rib, so you'd have to start timing it about twenty-eight minutes before I kicked the goal. But still, there was an excellent half hour in there.) Not when my first girlfriend, Cindy, gave me her grape juice box in third grade. None of those moments compared. This is the best thirty minutes of my life.

We finish our last song. Clarissa, Mel, and I are all drenched in sweat, and I can tell that they're also ranking this really high on their list of life experiences. What if every show is like this from now on?

"Thanks for being here!" I shout. "We're Fanged Grapefruit! Do you wanna hear one more?"

The crowd cheers.

The owner of the club points to his watch and shakes his head.

"I'm told that we can't play one more," I announce. "But we're here every Monday! Hope to see you again!"

The crowd cheers some more. I feel like they'd give us a standing ovation if they weren't already standing. And then they file toward the exit. That's right. They were here for us!

The lead singer of Bathtub Scum is standing in the corner, looking dismayed. "Where are they going? They're not leaving, are they? What about us? Doesn't anybody care about us? Why would they leave?" The other band members quietly console him as the club empties.

"Wow," says Clarissa.

"Yeah, wow," says Mel. "That was the best two minutes of my life."

"It was half an hour," I say.

"Felt like two minutes." Mel lets out a whoop. "They loved us! They loved us, right? I wasn't imagining that?"

"Nope, they loved us. I guess word finally got out." I can't stop grinning. I want to turn cartwheels and squeal with glee, but that would be unbecoming for the lead singer of a punk rock band.

The audience clears out of the club pretty quickly. Blake is also gone, which is nice. I don't want him coming over and spoiling my joyous feeling by doing something reprehensible.

It *does* seem kind of strange that all those people came into the club and didn't even stay for the headliner. I wonder what we did differently.

Maybe word got out of my alleged behavior in biology class. Maybe they hoped I'd do the same thing onstage. *You've gotta see Fanged Grapefruit! The lead singer chucks rat guts at the audience! It's wicked!*

Nah. It seems unlikely that childish behavior in biology class would pack the audience with an older crowd.

Did we get written up on a popular blog?

Did Audrey do some new social media promotion and not tell us?

As we break down the equipment, Clarissa asks, "Does it seem weird to anyone else that we had so many people?"

"A little," Mel admits.

"What do you think happened? We used the same fliers, right?" Clarissa works at a copy shop, and after we designed the "Fanged Grapefruit Is Performing at the Lane" flier, she printed up five hundred copies without her boss catching her. Each time we put some up, we cross out the old date and write in the new one.

"Yeah, same fliers," Mel says. "I didn't do anything different. Did you do anything different, Rod?"

"I didn't do anything different."

"Let's not overanalyze it," says Clarissa. "We had our best show ever, and we should just enjoy it."

"I agree," I say, although I'm suddenly not sure that I agree.

151

We finish breaking down the equipment and load everything into my car. I keep waiting for Blake to leap out of the shadows like a happiness-draining vampire.

Clarissa, Mel, Audrey, and I spend a couple of minutes talking about how awesome the show went. But my enthusiasm is starting to diminish.

"What's wrong?" Audrey asks me.

"What if Blake bribed the audience?"

Clarissa frowns. "You think Blake paid fifty people to be there?"

"I don't think it's out of the question."

We're all silent for a moment.

"Hmm," says Mel.

"Please don't say hmm. That sound has been ruined for me," I explain.

"Do you really think he'd do that?" Clarissa asks. "You guys can't stand each other, right? Why would he want to bring people to the show?"

"Maybe so that we can bask in the glory, and then he can crush our spirits by revealing that he bribed everyone."

"He definitely didn't bribe that first guy," says Mel. "That dude was totally rocking out."

"I bet he bribed everybody else though."

"That would suck," says Mel.

"I can't imagine that he would do that," says Clarissa. "Doesn't he have anything better to do than go around finding people to pay to attend a punk rock show?"

"No," I say. "He definitely does not."

"Maybe he asked them to show up but didn't actually pay anybody," Audrey offers.

"We've asked people to show up, and they almost never do."

"You think it's Blake's charisma?" asks Mel.

"No!" I say. "Everybody in this car is more charismatic than Blake! We could be hacking up hairballs and have more charisma. I can't believe you even said that."

"Some people like the guy. That's all I'm saying."

"Well, they're wrong."

"Let's say for the sake of argument that he did bribe them," says Audrey. "Is that such a bad thing?"

"Yes," I say.

"Maybe," Mel says.

"No," Clarissa says.

"You assume that he has bad intentions," says Audrey, "but maybe he's trying to mend fences. Or maybe he genuinely sees the potential of Fanged Grapefruit and wants everybody else to see it too."

"Our perfect night is tainted," I mutter.

"I disagree," says Clarissa. "It doesn't matter how we got an audience. All that matters is that they enjoyed themselves."

"How do we know he didn't *pay* them to pretend that they were enjoying themselves?" I ask.

"Ugh," says Clarissa.

The four of us are bummed out for the rest of the drive.

16.

AFTER DROPPING OFF Clarissa and Mel, it occurs to me that if Blake *didn't* bribe the audience members, then he has successfully ruined my night by making me *think* he did. If that's the case, then he's very, very good at this whole life-destroying thing. I have to give him credit for his skills.

Nah. He bribed 'em.

"I apologize for not believing you at school today," says Audrey.

"Do you believe me now?"

She hesitates. "I believe you more than I did at school."

"Audrey!"

"What? I still have trouble with the idea of him throwing rat guts in his own face! It doesn't compute for me!"

"So why are you even apologizing if you still don't believe me?"

"Because I feel bad."

"Well, you should."

"I just want you to consider the idea that if he brought in the audience, he did it out of kindness."

"He did it out of evil."

"Which makes more sense? That he convinced people to go to the show—through financial means or whatever—because he was trying to hurt you or because he was trying to help you?"

"The second one makes more sense," I admit. "And that's what Blake is counting on. That's how he operates. If he does things that make no logical sense, then I sound stupid when I accuse him of the truth. It's kind of genius, if you think about it. But maybe he's not a genius. Either one of those work. Whichever it is, I promise you that he doesn't have my best interest or the best interest of Fanged Grapefruit in mind."

"Okay," says Audrey.

"What did you mean by that?" I ask suspiciously.

"I meant okay."

"You said it in a weird way that doesn't make me think you meant it."

"Fine. So I didn't fully commit to the okay."

"Then don't commit to the okay. See if I care."

Audrey stares out the window for a minute. Then she turns back to me. "Blake made me promise not to tell, but

I'm going to anyway. You know those band shirts that a couple of people were wearing at the show?"

"Yeah."

"Blake bought them. He said he knew you didn't like having him around and that you'd be upset if you found out that he was promoting the show, but he said that he believed in Fanged Grapefruit and wanted to see it succeed, so he was going to do everything he could to help out."

"So he did bribe them!"

"He gave a few people an incentive to have a good time."

"I can't believe you kept Blake's secret from me!"

"I didn't. I blabbed it the same night he asked me not to tell. It's been, like, two hours."

"Well, this is wonderful. What a treat for me that you're working with my nemesis. Anything else I should know?"

"We'll talk about this more when you're calmer."

"Oh, goody. I can't wait to hear how else you betrayed me."

"I didn't betray you, Rod. I sold Blake a couple of shirts so that he could help you."

What about you, reader? Are you on Blake's side too? You probably think he's oh-so-charming! *Oh, that Blake, what a splendid lad! I think he should be the narrator of this book!* Is that what you want? Should I ask him to finish telling this story? We'll change the title to *Blake, Hero of All the Lands*, and I bet this book will win all kinds of awards and stay at the top of the *New York Times* bestseller list for seventy-plus weeks. It'll get turned into a major motion picture starring Chris Pratt as Blake, and I'll be played by a CGI ogre. And the reviews will say that the movie isn't as good as the book because Blake was such an engaging narrator that no movie, even one with Chris Pratt in the lead, can compare! Why am I even still here? I'm done. I'll switch to a completely different book while we wait for Blake to bring his magnetic personality to these pages.

"Aha!" said Dr. Rubick, the world's greatest private investigator. "I know who stole the diamond golden coin!"

"Who?" asked his befuddled assistant, Mr. Gout. "Who could it have been? I've wracked my brains, but I have nary an idea!"

"It was…" said Dr. Rubick, pointing to Madame Bloom, "her!"

"I guess that makes sense," said Mr. Gout, "since she's the only one in the mansion who's still alive."

"Yes, I stole the diamond golden coin!" Madame Bloom confessed.

"Are you going to explain your motive and how you did it?" asked Mr. Gout.

"No. I assumed Dr. Rubick was going to do that."

"Actually, I've got nothin'," said Dr. Rubick. "Usually, I'm pretty good at figuring these things out, but I've been under a lot of pressure lately, what with the stock market crash and all. And I was only half-paying attention to this particular case. Glad I got the culprit right this time though. A lot of innocent people are in prison because of my shoddy work." Dr. Rubick laughed. "Oh, to have a moral compass again!"

Hi. It's Rod. Still here? I want to apologize for my outburst. It was inappropriate. You've been kind enough to take this journey with me, and there's no excuse for lashing out at you in that manner. It won't happen again. I know that you loathe Blake as much as I do and want to see him punished.

Still friends?

No? We're not? Really?

But I apologized. I admitted that I was wrong and assured you that it would never happen again. What more do you want? Should I beg for your forgiveness? Should I throw myself onto the floor and grab your leg and plead with you to keep reading? Will that make you happy?

Fine. Whatever. There are billions of other books you can read, so we'll leave the second half of this one blank. You can make up your own story. Maybe something about a magical elf who goes on a quest to punch a goblin or something. Or I'll fill the rest of it with the word *derp*. Derp. Derp. Derp. Derp. Derp.

You think I won't fill the rest of the book with derp? Challenge accepted! Derp. Derp. Derp. Derp. Derp.

Good luck writing your book report now. What kind of themes are you going to analyze from that, huh? Derp. Derp. Derp. Derp. Derp.

No, *you're* being childish. Here, I'll mix it up. Dah-derp. Dah-derp. Dah-derp. Dah-derpy derp derp.

I can't do it. You've invested too much time into my adventure for me to stop telling it. You don't have to accept my previous apology. I understand. You're used to book narrators treating you with respect, and I was completely out of line. No excuses. I promise this won't happen again if there's a sequel.

What's that? You accept my apology after all?

Thanks. I really appreciate it. We're in this together. I'll even try to use fewer parenthetical asides from now on. (Just kidding.)

Now I forget where I left off. Hold on a second while I skim back.

Audrey was saying, "I didn't betray you, Rod. I sold Blake a couple of shirts so that he could help you."

I pull up alongside Audrey's house. There's still plenty more to say, but her father isn't the world's biggest Rod Conklin fan. And if it looks like we're arguing in the car or making out, he'll come out with a golf club.

"We'll talk about this tomorrow," I say.

Audrey nods and gets out of the car.

I'm actually not one hundred percent sure if I should be mad at her or not. Obviously, I'm glad she sold a couple of shirts, even if it was to Blake, but she should have told me about it immediately, right? Maybe? I don't know. I'll figure out my feelings later.

I crank up the car stereo to "vibrate the steering wheel" volume and drive home. Loud music makes everything better, except your hearing. I hope that Blake walked back from the Lane, which would get him home around 5:00 a.m., but when I walk inside, he's sitting on the living room couch.

"Great show!" he says.

"Bite me," I say.

Blake frowns. "That's kind of harsh. Did you think the show went poorly? Was that a smaller audience than usual?"

"You paid them all to be there."

"What are you talking about?"

"Forty-nine of those people were there because you bribed them."

"What a nutty thing to say."

"What's your plan this time, Blake? Why did you do it? What's your endgame?"

"I'm not sure where you came up with this conspiracy

theory, but all I did was offer a couple of suggestions that improved your performance. Maybe word got out that you were putting on a better show."

"Audrey told me what happened."

Blake adjusts himself on the cushion. "Did she now?"

"Yeah."

"And you believe her?"

"Of course I believe her."

"Over your own flesh and blood?"

"When that flesh and blood is you, yes, absolutely."

"I bought two T-shirts from her before the show, and I gave them to a couple of people. That's not a bribe. That's advertising. Everybody in that club was there of their own free will."

"I'm not saying you kidnapped or blackmailed them. I'm saying you bribed them."

"With what?"

"Money!" I shouted.

"I may have lots of money, but I wouldn't squander it on something like that. Not after what you did in biology class."

"I didn't do anything in—" Nope. Not gonna go there.

"If your girlfriend is making up some story about me paying people to go to your show, that's between you and her. I gave out a couple of free T-shirts. That's all."

"I don't believe you."

"If you'd rather believe that I bribed the audience instead of them showing up willingly for a top-notch musical performance, that's your own self-esteem issue. I choose to believe that Fanged Grapefruit is becoming a word-of-mouth sensation."

"You're not coming to the show next week."

"Why? I stood politely in the back. You're angry because you had five times the usual crowd? I'm sorry, Rod, but that's wacky."

When he puts it like that, it *does* sound wacky. But I believe Audrey over him, and I believe that Blake has sinister intent, even if I don't know what it is yet.

"We'll discuss it next week," I tell him.

Blake shrugs. "That's fair."

"He was incredible!" Blake says to Mom as we sit at the dinner table. "It's hard for me to even describe how much talent Rod and his friends have! I've seen some great shows in my life, but this was at a whole different level."

"I'm sorry I missed it," says Mom.

"You'll have literally thousands of other chances," says Blake. "This was no fluke. Fanged Grapefruit is here to stay."

Mom smiles. "Maybe they'll change the name before they make it big." Mom was never a big fan of the name Fanged Grapefruit.

"I don't get it," she said.

"It's a grapefruit with fangs."

"Is the grapefruit playing music?"

"No. It takes something that an average family would have for breakfast every morning and adds an element of danger. And it's a surreal image. Dangerous and surreal. That's us."

"What about Fanged Kiwi?"

"No."

"I still don't get it then," Mom said. "But I'm glad you are having fun."

"Oh, they can't change the name now," says Blake. "They've got name recognition. It's all about branding."

"Glad to hear the show went well," Mom tells me. "You certainly put in the hours practicing."

"He's a musical genius," says Blake. "I'm not saying that he'll be a millionaire by the time he's twenty, but twenty-two or twenty-three guaranteed."

"Good," says Mom. "I'm looking forward to retiring and living a life of luxury."

I'll be honest. I have plenty of dreams where my band is so successful that Mom can quit both of her jobs and spend her days relaxing on a beach sipping sparkling beverages while her full-time chocolate distributor feeds her bonbons. I don't like Blake inserting himself into these dreams.

Blake winks at me.

Grrrrr.

When I go in my room again, it looks like Blake's posters are another inch farther on my side. I'm sure it's an optical illusion. Or a problem with my brain.

I can't fall asleep on the air mattress, so I sleep out on the couch. I can still hear his snoring. Eighty-nine more days to go.

17.

I'M GOING TO compress time here and cover the next week like a montage in a movie. The montage will be accompanied by my soon-to-be smash hit single "The Ballad of Blake."

Got a cousin named Blake. (Blake! Blake!)
Yeah, a cousin named Blake. (Blake! Blake!)

Tuesday morning. Audrey walks up to my locker and says something. The background music drowns out her dialogue, but you can tell that she's apologizing. I say something that you also can't hear, but it looks like I'm reassuring her. The volume of the song fades for one line from me. "Blake said that you were lying to me."

Audrey looks surprised. Then she looks angry. Though Audrey is petite, you don't want to see her get angry.

I give her an expression that clearly indicates that we're

both in this together and that there's no way Blake will be able to drive us apart.

Audrey sighs and shakes her head.

Oh, I can't stand Blake.
Wanna throw him in a lake.
Abandon him during an earthquake.
Or deny him a slice of cake.

In English class Blake reads aloud from *Falling Leaves of the Life Tree.* Ms. Mayson nods approvingly at the sound of his melodic voice. The rest of the class follows along in the book, but I sit in my seat, scowling.

He keeps me awake.
And he's such a snake.
His face I'd like to break.
Hope he gets a toothache.

In biology class Blake walks over to our lab station and jokingly covers his face as if he thinks I'm going to fling something at him. I'm not amused.

Wish I didn't have a cousin named Blake. (Blake! Blake!)

*My life would be greatly improved without the existence of
my cousin named Blake. (Blake! Blake!)*

Wednesday morning. I drag myself off the couch,
exhausted from my lack of sleep. Close-up of the dark rings
under my eyes. How much longer can our hero take this?

He's a great big ol' fake.
Trust him? A mistake.
Think it's time to make.
A pointy wooden stake.

I'm in the cafeteria. They're serving tacos. Even Blake
does not have the power to diminish my enjoyment of them.

Hope he steps on a rake.
And spills his milkshake.
And gets an overcooked steak.
He's one I'd like to forsake.

Clarissa, Mel, and I are practicing in my garage. Clarissa
and Mel seem less annoyed that Blake is watching us than I
am. Close-up of Audrey, who seems to have the same level of
annoyance that I do.

I'd spend every day walking around with a big grin on my face and whistling merry tunes if not for my cousin named Blake. (Blake! Blake!)

Yeah, I'd be insufferable about my love for the world around me and my appreciation for all of the beauty in nature, but it's all messed up because of my cousin named Blake. (Blake! Blake!)

Thursday morning. When the alarm clock goes off, I'm so tired that I start to cry. (I didn't actually cry in real life, but it sounds more dramatic this way.)

I don't like you, Blake.
Really don't like you, Blake.
You're quite unlikable, Blake.
I'm just no fan of Blake.

Back in the cafeteria for lunch, Blake sits with several other kids. That's cool. I don't begrudge him making friends. The more people he has to hang out with, the less time he'll spend around me.

There are still other words that rhyme with Blake.
Like bake and Jake and slake and flake.

And spake and partake and remake and opaque.
But I think I'm done rhyming with Blake.

Fanged Grapefruit is practicing once again. Blake says something. Mel and Clarissa nod their approval. I'm not nodding. You can tell in my eyes that I do not approve of whatever he said.

[Unbelievably awesome guitar solo.]

Friday morning. The alarm goes off. I roll off the couch and land on the floor, where I remain unconscious for several minutes. (It's a long guitar solo.)

[Guitar solo continues.]

I walk through the school, bleary-eyed. The other students in the hallway fade away, which symbolizes how I feel all alone in the world. Bet you weren't expecting symbolism, huh? Then the students all reappear, so you know this isn't a book about a school full of kids who vanished into thin air.

Got a cousin named Blake. (Blake! Blake!)
Yeah, a cousin named Blake. (Blake! Blake!)

The final bell rings, ending another week of class. Audrey and I walk out of school together. You can tell from the lighting and the camera angle that we're perfect for each other.

Perfect for each other.
Ain't nothin' gonna mess that up.
Nope, nothin' can mess that up.
Certainly not my cousin.
We'll be together at least until the start of junior year.
Because nothin' gonna mess that up.
We're immune to any and all efforts to tear us apart.
I'm sure.
There's no way anything can go wrong in our relationship due to actions by somebody else.
'Cause we're perfect for each other.
I hope this song's not ironic.

18.

IT'S SATURDAY MORNING. Normally, that's my favorite morning of the week, but I'm almost delirious with exhaustion by this point. You'd think that I'd eventually be able to tune out Blake's snoring the same way that people who live next to a railroad stop hearing the trains, but his snoring operates on some bizarre frequency, so you can never get used to it. Soon I'll have to start making a bedtime ritual of knocking myself out with a brick.

I can't believe it was only last Saturday that I picked Blake up from the airport. That feels like eight thousand Saturdays ago.

Blake is not here. Some of his new friends invited him to go bowling. He woke me up when he left the house, but now that he's gone, I can sleep in for a few dozen more hours.

My phone vibrates. A text from Audrey. Call me!!!

Three exclamation points. There's no smiley face or

frowny face to give further information, so I assume all three of those exclamation points are good.

I call her. "Hey, what's up?" I ask.

She doesn't say anything. I can hear her sniffle on the other end. Unless she's been kidnapped by somebody with a cold and they are calling for ransom, but that seems unlikely.

"Rod?" she asks, sounding like she's been crying. Oh, jeez, I hope her pet boa constrictor didn't die. (Yep, she has a pet boa constrictor. I would've mentioned it earlier, but I didn't want to sound like I was bragging by telling you that my girlfriend has a pet boa constrictor.)

"What's wrong?" I'm worried about Audrey and her pet snake.

"Do you still care about me?"

That is one loaded question. Fortunately, the truth and the correct answer are the same. "Of course!"

"Are you sure?"

"Yes, I'm sure. What happened?"

"Why are you writing poems for Gretchen McCoy?"

Because of my exhaustion, my initial thought is, *That's funny. I don't recall writing any poems for Gretchen McCoy. I wonder what they said.* Then I realize that I don't remember writing them because I never wrote Gretchen any poems. *Blake!*

"What do you mean?" I ask suspiciously.

"Gretchen told me that you slipped several love poems into her locker."

"Were they any good?"

"I don't know. She didn't read them to me."

"I don't write poetry, Audrey. I write song lyrics."

"Sometimes your lyrics are poetic."

"Not many of them. You know this has to be Blake's doing, right?"

"Why would he do that?"

"Why does Blake do anything? Did Gretchen say these poems were in my handwriting?"

"She said they were printed out from a computer."

"Were they in my favorite font?"

Audrey sniffles. "I didn't ask."

"I promise you it was Blake. He probably wrote some love poems and slipped them into Gretchen's locker, knowing that Gretchen would tell you about them instead of coming to me first. I'd never write poems and sign my name to them. That would be stupid. First of all, I wouldn't write another girl love poems, and second of all, if I wrote you a love poem, I'd want you to know it was from me."

"She said they weren't signed but that there were various clues that made it clear they came from you."

"Okay, so Blake is too clever to add a fake signature. I

didn't write them. You can tell Gretchen that she was set up. But let her down easy. I mean, don't make her cry or anything. Tell her that if I weren't completely devoted to you, I'd probably write some song lyrics for her, but since you're the only girl for me, she'll have to find somebody else."

"I'll figure out a different way to phrase that," says Audrey. I can hear her blow her nose. "I'm sorry. I got so upset that I wasn't thinking straight. Of course it was Blake."

"I'll confront him when he's done bowling."

"Good."

"Ask her if the poems were any good though. I'm interested to hear if he has talent."

"He probably copied them from somewhere."

"You're right," I say. "Scumbag plagiarist."

"I'm going to call Gretchen."

"Let me know how it goes."

Apparently, Gretchen was relieved that the poems didn't come from me, which hurts my feelings a little bit.

Clearly, Blake has stepped up his evil game. Too bad for him. It'll take a lot more than some misattributed love poems to drive Audrey and me apart.

Audrey calls around noon. She's crying again.

"What's wrong?" I ask.

"Do you have a crush on Bernadette Springer?"

"Who?" That is absolutely the wrong answer. I know who Bernadette Springer is. She's the head of the cheerleading squad. If you picture the ugliest person you've ever seen in your life and then picture their exact opposite, that's Bernadette. My knee-jerk reaction of "Who?" was a terrible because it sounds like I'm lying. I guess I was. It's just that when my girlfriend asks me if I have a crush on somebody, no matter who it is, my reaction is going to be "Who?" because I only have eyes for her. Judge me however you wish.

"Bernadette Springer. Head of the cheerleading squad. You know her. Everybody knows her."

"Oh, right. Her." Yes, I pretend that it took me a moment to place her name. I'm completely innocent of the crime of having a crush on Bernadette, but I get flustered when being interrogated, okay? "Of course I don't have a crush on her."

"Then why were you with her at the Lane last night?"

"I wasn't!"

"I heard that you were talking to her for forty-five minutes and that you looked like you had a total crush on her."

"Who told you this?"

"Daryn Jonas."

"And who told him this?"

"I don't know."

"The Lane is an eighteen-and-over club on Friday nights. I couldn't go in there even if I wanted to."

"I think he meant that you two were standing outside the Lane."

"C'mon, Audrey, do you really honestly believe that Bernadette Springer would talk to me for forty-five minutes?"

If you're grading my answers thus far, "Who?" was a D+ graded on a curve, while this was an F. Because it implies that Audrey, who has spoken with me for far longer than forty-five minutes over the course of our relationship, is an easier catch than Bernadette.

Do I try to course-correct by saying something like "That's not what I meant!" or do I hope that Audrey doesn't interpret my response in the same way?

I go with the latter.

"What do you mean by that?" she asks.

Wrong choice.

"Nothing," I say, which is the wrong answer.

"I know I'm not as pretty as her," says Audrey.

"Yes, you are," I insist. "Bernadette has a face like a pug compared to you." That was probably too much of an over-correction. I should've gone with some variety of terrier.

"So as soon as your band starts to be successful, you talk to other girls?"

"No! I haven't said two consecutive sentences to Bernadette the entire time we've been in high school. I'm not sure who Daryn heard that from or who that person heard it from, but the chain begins with Blake."

"Did you confront him about the poems?"

"He's not back from bowling yet."

"How many games is he bowling?"

"I don't know. Maybe it takes him a long time to get a bowling ball all the way down the lane."

Audrey is quiet for a moment. "Yeah, I guess it probably was Blake who started the rumor."

"There's nothing to guess. It was definitely him. Why would you even think otherwise?"

"Well, you had a really good show on Monday, and singers get lots of chicks…"

"You're the only chick I want."

"Okay."

"If you hear any other rumors, I'm sure they can be traced back to my cousin. I would never let fame change me, change us."

"Okay. I'm sorry," Audrey says and sniffles again.

I get a text from Audrey: Call me. No exclamation points. I'm not sure if that's better or worse. I'm going to assume worse.

"Hey," I say.

"Have you been texting Lorelei Michaels?"

"Are you kidding me?"

"She showed me texts of you asking her out. You said we'd broken up."

"Wait. She showed them to you?"

"Yes."

"Hold on." I check my texts. There's nothing to or from Lorelei. "Are you sure they're from my phone?"

"It's your number."

"Blake must have swiped my phone and then deleted everything when he was done."

"Don't you have a passcode?"

"Yeah, but the passcode is my birthday."

"How would he get your phone?"

"He lives in my house! He could've done it while I was asleep or in the shower. I had no idea he'd go this far to sabotage me."

"Is he still bowling?"

"He hasn't come back from bowling, but I assume he's done by now. There's only so long you can bowl."

"I wish this would stop," says Audrey.

"Me too." Then I unwisely decide to add some levity to the conversation. "So did Lorelei say…" I'm four words into my five-word sentence when I realize that this is not the appropriate time to make a joke, and although my brain frantically waves a stop sign, my mouth drives right through it. "Yes?"

"Is that a joke?" Audrey asks.

"Yeah," I say. "I was trying to relieve the tension."

"Leave the tension where it is."

"Sorry. I will," I say, and I mean it.

"But, no, Lorelei did not say yes. She asked why you were asking her out when you already had a girlfriend. Your text explained that things hadn't been going well between us for a while and that while you didn't officially break up with me, we both understood that it was over and that we were free to—"

"Reminder," I say, "this is what Blake said, not me."

"Right," says Audrey.

"Right," I say, more firmly.

"I know."

"I sure hope you know. You mean the world to me, Audrey."

"It's just…"

"It's just what? Blake did this. That's the only explanation that should be running through anybody's mind right now."

"It's just that this is a lot."

"I know. What's his deal?"

"He had to write all those poems for Gretchen and then spread a rumor about you talking to Bernadette and then steal your phone to text Lorelei," says Audrey. "It's a lot."

"It *is* a lot. I've been saying that since I first picked him up at the airport. He's an unusual character."

"Maybe you should call the police."

"Whoa. My mom would freak if I called the cops on him, and I don't think he's committed an actual crime, even if he's a pain."

"He stole your phone to text another girl."

"That's more of a prank than a misdemeanor," I say. "I'm not calling the police. If I wake up and he's hovering over me with a butcher knife and a creepy mask, yeah, then I'll call 911."

You know what's scary? I can actually picture Blake hovering over me with the knife, and it doesn't seem like a ridiculous mental image! Granted, in my imagination he's wearing a cat mask, so I can't see his face, but I know it's him.

Am I afraid of my cousin?

Nah. Blake isn't frightening. He's just a jerk.

I hope.

"I'm sorry," says Audrey. "I don't know why Blake is

trying to ruin our relationship. Make sure you confront him when he gets back from bowling, okay?"

"I will. I promise."

A new text from Audrey: Call me? I have no idea how to interpret the question mark. I'm pretty sure she's not going to say, "Hi, Rod, wanted to let you know that all our problems have been solved! Bye-bye!"

"What did he do this time?" I ask when she picks up.

"I got a picture of your car parked outside of Shannon Calmone's house last night."

"How do you know it was my car?"

"I know what your car looks like."

"How do you know it was last night?"

"The phase of the moon in the picture is correct."

"So it could have been last month?"

"I guess."

Wait. Why am I arguing lunar cycles? I've never parked my car in front of Shannon's house. "That wasn't me," I insist. "He must've stolen my car and parked it there."

"Do you really think he could steal your car keys, sneak out of the house, drive over to Shannon's, take the picture, drive back home, sneak back into the house, and slip your keys back where he found them without getting caught?"

"You're making it sound really complicated with all those steps, but sure, why not? It would've taken twenty minutes, tops."

"How do you know how far away Shannon lives?"

"I went to a birthday party when she turned eight or something." I suddenly remember that it was her ninth birthday, not her eighth, but if I correct myself, it'll look like I'm floundering to make up a story on the spot. "Blake could've easily done this."

"Do you really think he'd take the risk of getting caught?"

"Considering the things he's said to my face without worrying that I'd beat him up, yes, I think he'd take the risk. He'd come up with some story about how he needed cough syrup or something and didn't want to wake us up going through the medicine cabinets to find some, so he borrowed my car to drive to the twenty-four-hour pharmacy. And you know what? He probably really did buy some cough syrup so that if I called him a liar, he could whip out the bottle and say, 'See, here it is.' Or maybe the picture is Photoshopped. He seems like somebody who'd be good at Photoshop. Do you know any experts who could vouch for the authenticity of the picture?"

"No."

"It's either a picture of my stolen car, or it's fake. Either way, I most definitely was not parked outside of Shannon's house last night. With Blake's snoring, I'm not getting enough sleep to be out gallivanting at night." I think of something funny to say about that, but having learned from previous mistakes, I keep my mouth shut.

"Hold on," Audrey says. A moment later she speaks again, "I got a new picture."

"Of what?"

"You sharing a french fry with Melissa Ruggarth."

"Oh." I know that picture. "That one might be legit."

Melissa and I were getting a burger and fries. One of the fries in my bag was so long that we each started eating one side of the fry, and somebody took a picture. It's actually kind of adorable, though I do not describe it as such to Audrey.

"Why were you sharing a fry with Melissa?"

"It was last year before we were dating. Look at my hair."

"Your hair looks the same as it does now."

"Really?"

"Yes."

"Then my hair is Photoshopped. Which is good, because

now we know that Blake is digitally manipulating the pictures and didn't actually steal my car."

"Are you really trying to convince me that Blake Photoshopped your hair to make a picture from last year look more recent?"

"Yes! And I shouldn't have to convince you of this! You should be saying, 'Yep, that's the next phase of Blake's plan.' We're supposed to be teaming up against him."

"What you're saying doesn't make any sense."

"What makes more sense? That I'm suddenly going after Gretchen, Bernadette, Lorelei, Shannon, and Melissa?"

"You did have a really good show. It could have boosted your confidence."

"Ask Melissa. She'll tell you that we shared the french fry a year ago."

"Why am I only hearing about it now?"

"Because...because...because it's a fry! One fry! A year ago! It was an amusing picture!"

"I wasn't amused by it."

"Look, I feel like there's a cloud of paranoia forming over you, and that's exactly what Blake wants. He's trying to tear us apart. We can't let him succeed."

"I guess not," says Audrey.

I can't believe this. Blake's plan is *working*. I could defend myself against any one of these false accusations, but the sheer volume is wearing Audrey down.

"You should come over," I say. "You need to see the sincerity in my eyes."

"Okay."

"I'll come get you."

"No, I could use a bike ride. I'm leaving now."

We hang up.

I have no idea how Blake thinks he can get away with this. None of these lies are going to hold up.

Unless he has a history of bribing people. Oh, wait…

I won't worry about that for now.

And I won't worry about losing Audrey. Once she has a moment to think about it (and as mentioned before, the opportunity to see the sincerity in my eyes), she'll realize that it's all a big con. I didn't do anything wrong.

In the end, this is all for the best. If Blake is doing awful things to purposely destroy my relationship with Audrey, Mom won't let him stay with us. Aunt Mary and Uncle Clark will just have to come back from Antarctica or Middle Earth or wherever their cruise ship is currently docked and collect their miserable excuse for a son.

It's all going to be fine.

There's a knock at the door.

It's too soon for that knock to have come from Audrey, unless she was standing in my yard the whole time we were talking on the phone.

I peek out the window. It's not Audrey or Blake. It's Jennifer Render. You don't know who she is, but if you've been paying attention during this chapter, you can probably figure out how she fits into the overall puzzle.

This ain't good.

19.

MAYBE I SHOULD pretend I'm not home.

This would be a brilliant idea, except that Jennifer saw me peeking out the window. She smiles and waves.

Okay, clearly, Blake has arranged for Jennifer to be here when Audrey arrives, so Audrey can say, "What is *she* doing here?" and I can say, "No, no, it's not what it looks like!" and Jennifer can say, "But I thought you two had broken up!" and Audrey can storm off in tears.

That might be pushing it. That scenario would require Blake to know that I was going to suggest that Audrey come over to my house and then to send Jennifer over at the perfect time. Although, technically, this isn't the *perfect* time. Jennifer's here early enough that I can probably send her on her way before Audrey arrives. Still, Blake being able to coordinate the situation so well puts him into the "omniscient supervillain" category, and I don't want to give him that much credit.

I should hide. What's Jennifer going to do? Break down the door? Even if she starts pounding on it and shouting, "I know you're in there, Rod!" surely she'll get bored and leave before Audrey gets here, right?

The word *surely* should be purged from my vocabulary. Nothing is working out the way it should.

I open the door. Jennifer, still smiling, gives her head an alluring tilt. "Hi, Rod."

"Hi, Jennifer." I consider pretending that I don't remember her name, but we have two classes together. Though we've never socialized outside of school, I know perfectly well that her name is Jennifer. If I want to get out of this predicament (Fun fact: I do), it's best for me to stick to the truth.

"How's it going?" she asks.

I shrug. "Eh." I can't say it's been a great day.

"Just eh?"

"Yeah. Below eh, actually."

"I'm sorry to hear that. I heard your band had a really amazing show Monday night."

"Yep."

"I didn't even know you were in a band." She giggles. "Are you keeping secrets from me, Rod Conklin?"

Okay, yeah, she's definitely working for my cousin. "How much did Blake pay you?" I ask.

"I don't know what you're talking about. Who's Blake?"

"My cousin Blake. There was an incident between us during biology class."

Jennifer nods. "Oh, yeah. I heard about that. He totally deserved it. He's lucky you didn't do worse."

"I didn't do anything."

"That was very restrained of you."

"Blake's out of control. He's trying to ruin my relationship with Audrey."

"You're in a relationship with Audrey?" Jennifer asks. "I had no idea. Lucky girl."

"Seriously. He's the bad guy here, and if you're on his side, you're on the wrong side of history."

"I don't know him at all."

"Then why are you here?"

"Because it sounds like you're about to become really popular." She leans closer to me. "And I want to be on the right side of history."

This would be a terrible, terrible moment for Audrey to show up, and fortunately, she doesn't. "Well, I know he paid you, so…"

"Nobody paid me."

"Bribed you."

"Nobody bribed me."

"Blackmailed?" Has Blake really gone that far?

"I'm here because I want to get to know you better. No other reason."

"Yeah, right."

"Yeah, wrong."

"What does that even mean?"

Jennifer's smile disappears. "I don't appreciate your attitude."

"And I don't appreciate you being Blake's pawn. So it's time to leave. Rapidly."

Jennifer folds her arms in front of her chest. "I'm not going anywhere until you apologize."

"I apologize. Bye."

"You're a jerk."

"No, *Blake* is a jerk. I'm the victim of a jerk."

"Why don't you like me?"

"I like you fine. But I already have a girlfriend. Now go."

Should I slam the door in her face? She's standing a little too close. I don't want to break her nose. You don't get to claim you're the good guy after you break a girl's nose.

"All right," says Jennifer. "I'll leave."

Jennifer does not leave.

"Now?" I suggest.

"Sure."

"So…"

"Yes?"

"You haven't left."

"Oh."

"You were supposed to."

"I'm getting around to it."

"Get around to it faster."

"There's no need to be rude."

"Apparently, there *is* a need to be rude."

"Most guys aren't in a hurry to send me away."

"This is an unusual circumstance."

"May I come in and use your bathroom?"

"No."

"Rude."

"Sorry." I shrug.

"I really, really have to go to the bathroom."

"Sorry."

"I'll wet my pants right here on your front porch," she says.

"You know what? If that's the way things are heading, there's nothing I can do about it. I'd prefer you not wet your pants on my porch, but if I have to choose between that and letting you inside, then I'm afraid I have to go with the pants-wetting option. Nothing personal."

Jennifer glares at me. "Everybody says that you're a gentleman. I guess they were wrong."

"Nobody says I'm a gentleman," I insist.

"Everybody does."

"No, they don't. They might say I'm a cool punk rocker, but not a gentleman."

"Nobody says you're a cool guy."

"Nobody?" This news is somewhat distressing.

"Nope."

"You're trying to hurt my feelings."

"I help feelings. I don't hurt them."

"You need to go."

"I agree with you."

"I know what you're doing. You're avoiding leaving so that you're here when Audrey gets here."

Jennifer looks a little worried. "Is Audrey on her way?"

"Yes. You didn't know that?"

"How would I know that?"

"Because you're here because of Blake."

"No, I'm not."

"Of course you are."

"I barely know him. He's not somebody I'd do favors for."

"So you're admitting that you know him a little."

"Barely."

"That's enough."

"Enough for what?"

"To be bribed or blackmailed."

"You live in a weird world."

"If you're not working with Blake, why are you here?"

"I already said. To get to know you better."

"Right, but now you know that I have a girlfriend and that she's on the way over, and you're still standing there. Your reasoning no longer holds up."

Jennifer puts her hand on her hip. "Maybe I think I can compete with her."

"I'm not going to comment on that either way, but it's obviously not why you're here. Just admit it."

"Will you let me use your bathroom if I admit it?"

"No."

"Rude."

"Am I going to have to call the police?"

"Are you the kind of guy who'd call the police on a girl who wanted to ask him out?"

"I'm moving in that direction."

"Do you want to go to the movies tonight?"

"Can't."

"Why not?" She looks insulted.

"Because I have a girlfriend and you don't really mean it."

"What makes you say that?"

"Could you step back a bit?" I ask.

"Sure."

Jennifer doesn't step back. I can't slam the door unless she steps back. Even you wouldn't sympathize with me if I broke her nose.

"You're not stepping back," I say.

"I thought I did."

"Nope."

"Pretty sure I did."

"Nope."

"My feet look like they're in a different spot."

"Nope. Your feet are exactly where they were before."

"Interesting."

Audrey could be here any minute. If Jennifer *still* refuses to leave and continues playing dumb, that might work to my benefit because Audrey would immediately realize that Jennifer isn't really here to get to know me better. But if Jennifer sees her and hurries away, it could be problematic.

You know what I should do? I should give Audrey a heads-up that Jennifer is standing on my front porch and won't leave. That way she won't be ruled by emotion when she gets here.

I tap my cell phone screen.

"Are you playing Candy Crush?" Jennifer asks.

"No."

"Who are you texting?"

"I'm not texting."

"Who are you calling?"

"Audrey."

"Why?"

"To let her know you're here."

For a second, I think Jennifer is going to slap my phone out of my hand. (Or at least try. I have a firm grip.) But she doesn't.

The phone rings a few times then goes to voicemail.

"She didn't answer?" asks Jennifer.

"No."

"She must not care about you."

"She's riding a bike."

"So?"

"She might not have noticed that I called. Or she did notice but didn't want to stop to answer because she's on her way over here and will see me soon anyway."

"She can't talk and ride a bike?"

"She can't ride a bike and take her cell phone out of her pocket and answer it, no."

"She sounds unskilled."

"Please don't insult my girlfriend."

"I apologize."

"You could make it up to me by telling the truth about Blake."

"There's nothing to tell."

"What's going on?"

Guess who said that? Correct!

"Oh, hi," Jennifer says to Audrey. "Do you know Rod, Audrey?"

Audrey gets off her bicycle and lets it fall onto my lawn. "Yes, I do."

"She knows you know me," I say. "We were literally just talking about you being my girlfriend."

"I have no idea what he's talking about," says Jennifer. I'm kind of relieved that she's lying right to my face. I now know for certain that she's helping Blake and that I wasn't simply being rude to a girl who wanted to get to know the lead singer of a punk rock band on the rise.

"Did Blake send you?" Audrey asks.

"Blake who?"

"She knows who Blake is," I say.

"Did Blake send you?" Audrey asks again.

"Blake Lively? Blake Shelton? William Blake?"

"William Blake has been dead for two hundred years."

(Audrey says this. She knows more than I do about the life and death of English poets and visual artists of the Romantic Age who lived during the late eighteenth and early nineteenth century.)

"I meant a different William Blake."

"I'm talking about Blake Montgomery," Audrey clarifies.

"Don't know him," says Jennifer.

"Rod's cousin."

"Still don't know him."

"I have pictures of you talking to him."

"No, you don't."

Wouldn't it have been great if this made Jennifer break down and confess? We could've wrapped this book up a few chapters earlier.

Audrey steps up onto the porch.

"Anyway," says Jennifer, "I can see that there's about to be a spat, so I'm going to head home. If you two work it out, great, but if not, Rod, you know where to find me."

Jennifer walks away. I hope that Audrey's angry expression is meant for her, that maybe she's trying to decide whether or not to leap on her back and tackle her to the ground, but I quickly discover that the expression is all mine.

"So let's analyze this," I say. "This is the fifth or sixth similar incident today. That's already defying credibility. And even if Jennifer wanted to get to know me better for real, she wouldn't show up at my house unannounced."

"I don't know why she was here," says Audrey, "and I don't know if she was announced or not."

"I told you to come over! It was my idea! Why would I invite you over if I knew Jennifer was on her way?"

"To make it easier to break up with me?"

"*What?*"

"I ride over here, see you with her, scream a little, slap you, and say I never want to see you again. It lets you off the hook."

"Okay," I say, "I can't be in a relationship if we're not even going to pretend to be on the same plane of reality."

"I know you say it was all Blake's doing, and it probably was. But maybe he was just speeding up the process."

"What are you talking about?"

"How long do you really think we were going to be together?"

"Longer than this!"

"It was never going to work out. You want to tour with a band, and I want to be an astronaut. We'd never see each other."

I'm so flabbergasted that I want to drop to the floor and roll around in circles and scream, "Gaaahhhhh!" But that's not how I want Audrey to remember me.

"I…can't…I…don't…I…can't…I…huh?" I say with maximum eloquence.

"I can't handle this dynamic anymore. Not for a relationship that was doomed from the first moment we met, when I asked if you knew where the gym was."

"But I did know where the gym was! And I'll always give you directions to the gym."

"I'm sorry, Rod."

"No. I do not accept this. If we're destined to break up, I don't want Blake to get the credit."

Audrey gives me a hug. Then she wipes a tear from her eye and walks away.

No.

Nooo.

Nooooooooooooooooooo!

"I thought we were going to defeat him together!" I shout.

She picks up her bicycle and rides away.

I stand there in shock for…I dunno, three minutes or so? I'm in too much shock to say for certain.

He did it. That wormy little weasel successfully nuked my relationship with Audrey. All I can say is that he'd better not bring home a bowling ball because his nose will be the headpin and I'm ready to bowl a strike.

That would make a great song lyric.

Your nose is the headpin, and I'm gonna bowl a—

No, that's an awful lyric. I can't even write songs anymore.

I resist the urge to cry. If I start bawling or even let a single manly tear trickle down my cheek, Blake will pick that moment to come home.

I wanna shed some tears, but I can't let you see me shedding.

Argh! My lyric-writing days are over! Over!

A car pulls up in front of my house, and Blake gets out. The car has tinted windows, so I can't see the driver. Maybe it's somebody I know. Maybe it's a crime lord. Or maybe it's an Uber driver.

Blake looks at my scowling face and grins. "How was your day? I guess we have a lot to talk about, huh?"

20.

I SAID THAT I was going to have a flashback to how Audrey and I met. It's too painful for me to do it now and kind of pointless seeing as how we've broken up. You probably got the idea that she was new in school and asked me for directions to the gym. Did she really not know where it was, or was it an excuse to talk to me because she'd heard I was in a band? I was going to ask her on our wedding day. Now it's a mystery for the ages.

Back to Blake. He walks toward the front door. Even though he has to know there's a strong possibility that I'm going to let out a battle cry and charge at him, he's not moving like somebody who expects to be attacked. I'll have to be cautious. He may have a can of mace.

"You suck," I tell him.

"May I explain myself?"

"Yeah, but you're not going to be successful."

"To answer the question that's on your mind, yes, I'm the reason Audrey broke up with you."

I attack.

If a college scout saw this tackle, they'd immediately offer me a football scholarship, and I would begin an exciting new era of my life. Sadly, there are no scouts to witness this amazing feat. We both hit the ground hard, and I hope that Blake landed on a spot of grass that's laden with fire ants, millions of enraged fire ants going *sting, sting, sting* until his back swells up like a water balloon.

Don't worry. I'm not going to do anything *too* violent. I'm still fully in control of my temper. I'm going to rough him up a little, maybe generate a few small bruises, but he won't end up in the hospital or anything like that.

Okay, yeah, I do throw a punch at his face. He blocks it though and rolls on top of me.

Suddenly, I am the one whose back is vulnerable to fire ants. Wait. Blake is *winning* this fight?

Yep. He sure is.

He's got me pinned to the ground, and my best efforts to break free are an embarrassing failure. If the football scout walks by now, I won't even get an offer to be the towel boy. ("Sorry, Mr. Conklin. Better luck next year.")

I am really, really, really surprised to be losing, but I suppose it makes sense. If you're as unlikable as Blake, you'd learn to defend yourself.

"Let me go!" I snarl.

"Stop snarling first."

"Let me go, or I'll scream!"

You now know that my account of these events is one hundred percent accurate because I would've otherwise left out the part where I said to let me go or I'd scream.

"Are you ready to discuss this calmly?" Blake asks.

"No!"

Blake slaps me across the face. Not hard enough to expose skull, but hard enough to remind me that I should be ashamed of how I'm faring in this fight.

"Are you ready now?" he asks.

"Getting closer."

Blake slaps me again. This one is an extremely light slap, clearly designed to send the message that I'm losing so badly that he doesn't need to make any further efforts to subdue me.

I land a punch to his jaw. Then I immediately apologize. Not for hurting him, but because it was such a weak, inept punch that it's an insult for me to have even thrown it. I can't even pretend that I did it that way on purpose. That was one shameful punch.

Blake does that trick where he mimics plucking my nose off my face and then pretends that his thumb is my nose, though he stops short of saying, "Got your nose!"

I throw another punch that completely misses, even though Blake is right on top of me and I shouldn't have been able to miss even if I had Tyrannosaurus rex arms.

"Are you going to make me honk your nose?" asks Blake.

"Maybe!"

"I don't want to do it."

I struggle to regain the upper hand in this war. I fail.

"Please don't make me honk your nose," says Blake. "You don't deserve that."

I continue to struggle. Surely, this time I'll successfully… Nope.

I have to surrender. I could survive the nose-steal fakeout, but if word gets out that my cousin honked my nose during combat, I'll have no friends left.

Or I could *pretend* to surrender, wait for him to lower his defenses, and then strike!

Nah, that's tacky.

"I give up," I say.

"You sure?"

"Yes." Especially because Audrey might change her mind and ride back to my house to un–break up with me, in which case, she'd see Blake giving me a fierce whupping and then leave again, feeling most disappointed in me.

"Good." Blake stands. I hope he doesn't extend a hand to

help me up because that will increase my level of humiliation by two or three degrees, but of course, he does. I let him help me up in a show of comradery.

We take a moment to catch our breath, by which I mean *I* take a moment to catch my breath while Blake waits patiently.

"What were we talking about again?" he asks.

"You drove Audrey away from me."

"Right. That."

"Why'd you do it?"

"Would you believe me if I said I was trying to help you?"

"Probably not."

"Well, I was."

"So if I were sinking in quicksand, you'd help by driving over me with a Humvee?"

"Did you—"

"Hold on," I say. I brush some ants and grass off my back. I pull up my shirt and turn around. "Are there any more?"

"A few. Want me to take care of them?"

"Yeah."

Blake brushes my back.

"I think there's one in my armpit," I say.

"I'm not touching that one."

I remove the pit ant myself and lower my shirt. "Thanks."

"Anytime."

"You were saying?"

"Did you see the way the ladies were looking at you during the show?"

"No," I say. "I was focused on the music like a professional."

"Well, I saw them."

"How? You were standing in the back."

"I walked around the club a little."

"I didn't see you move."

"Do you want me to prove it?" Blake asks. "Do you want to send the bottom of my shoes to forensics? I assure you that there are substances on those soles that you won't find anywhere else in the world."

"Fine. You saw girls looking at me. So what?"

"Didn't you get into music for the girls?"

"No. I got into music because I love punk rock."

"Girls had nothing to do with it?" he questions.

"They were on the list of reasons, but maybe in second or third place, not first. I'll say second place. Love of music and then girls…and then rebellion."

Blake nods. "So while it didn't make the top spot, the fact that females are attracted to members of successful musical acts was at least one of the fringe benefits of the business, correct?"

"Sure."

"As long as you were with Audrey, you couldn't partake in that benefit! All these ladies throwing themselves at you, and you had to say, 'Oh, goodness, no, I couldn't possibly make out with you!' What a waste!"

"It wasn't a waste. Audrey is awesome."

"She is, but when you're twenty-two years old and looking back on your life, will you be glad that you were locked into Audrey or glad that you were a free man? I don't think you would have untied the leash without my help. It was harsh. It was painful, and it was a little ugly. But now you are free to embrace the life of a punk rock superstar."

"Know what else you could have done?" I ask. "You could've sent me a text listing the benefits of not having a girlfriend and let me use that information to make my own, informed decision."

Blake shakes his head. "You wouldn't have done it. You needed somebody like me to give you a push."

"I need somebody like you the way I need scabies."

"I didn't expect you to understand right away."

I want to punch him again, but if it goes the way my first punch did, my morale will be so low that I'll flop onto the lawn and let the fire ants do with me what they will.

"Well, you got what you wanted," I say.

"No, I got you what you needed."

"Stop psychoanalyzing me."

"You'll thank me. I promise."

I'm pretty sure I won't, but I'm tired of arguing. Blake has now won so many rounds that I've lost count. I long for the simpler, more innocent times of a week ago when my greatest concern was that Mom was going to have to work overtime to pay extra to feed Rod. (See chapter one.) Even if I could have envisioned a world in which an evil cousin would attempt to destroy my relationship with my girlfriend, I never would have imagined that he'd succeed!

"I'm going inside," I say.

"For what?"

"To mope."

"Don't mope yet," says Blake. "I wouldn't take something away from you without giving back in return. Text Clarissa and Mel. Tell them to come over."

"Why? So you can make it look like I've been cheating on them with other bands?"

"I have good news."

"No news is good news coming from you."

"What do you mean?" asks Blake. "Is that a variation on 'No news is good news,' or do you mean that any news coming from me would be bad by definition?"

"The second one."

"I guarantee that this is the best news you've had all week."

"That's a low bar. You could tell me that I've got the stomach flu, and it would be the best news of the week."

"Let me correct myself. It's probably the best news you've had all year, but I've only been around you for the past week, so I don't want to overpromise."

"Go away."

"Tell them to come over. If it's not worth your while, you can break both of my arms."

"I'd love that, but I'd get in trouble with my mom."

"No, I'd let you break my arms, and then I'd make up a cover story. Two broken arms, free and clear. Think about it."

I shake my head. "Nah. I don't think I'd even enjoy it."

"I'd let you use a shovel."

"Nope."

"You sure? Broken arms hurt."

"I'd have to carry your books around all day and stuff. And you know what? I don't believe you when you say that you'd make up a cover story. I think I'd break your arms and you'd have hired private investigators to witness the entire thing, and then you'd get my room all to yourself because I'd be in jail. So no deal."

"Well, the point wasn't that you'd actually break my arms. The point was that you *wouldn't* break my arms because you'd realize that it had been a good idea to call Clarissa and Mel over here. If you can't even comprehend that this might be true, then I understand. I'll just talk to them myself."

"No. Stay away from my friends."

"They're my friends too."

"No, they're not. They're your mortal enemies. I don't want you calling them or texting them or following them on social media or putting any funny filters on pictures they post or having any interaction with them. As far as you're concerned, they don't exist. Got it?"

"You're endearing when you set boundaries."

"Got it?" I repeat.

"You know, Rod, I'm not big on telling people about the consequences they will face if they defy me. But if Clarissa and Mel find out that you purposely tried to keep this news from them, they'll never forgive you. That's all I'm saying."

"Stop trying to be a supervillain."

"I'm not."

"You are! Knock it off! Best-case scenario, you're a super-villain's lame sidekick."

"Are you going to call them over?"

This doesn't sound like a good idea. Why should I trust

Blake? He has literally proven himself to be the least trust-worthy person I know, and I knew this kid in third grade who kept promising that he wouldn't throw my ice cream cone on the ground if I handed it to him. And yet on three separate occasions, I let him hold my ice cream cone, and he did, in fact, throw it on the ground. I realize that this particular incident reflects badly on my judgment. (I mean, nobody asks to hold your ice cream cone for a selfless purpose.) But what I'm saying is that I trust Blake less than I trust the kid who kept saying, "C'mon, let me hold your ice cream cone. I won't throw it on the ground. I promise."

Still...

I know what you're thinking. "No! No 'Still...' 'Still...' is a terrible direction for your mind to be moving. The man cannot be trusted!"

But there's a small part of me that wants to believe that Blake might actually have good news to deliver. Don't get me wrong. I'm still furious about what he did to Audrey. Yet if you believe the reason he said he did it, it kind of makes sense, right? I'm not saying that I wanted to break up with her. That's not what I'm saying at all. Please don't stop reading this book because you've suddenly lost sympathy for the narrator. That's not remotely the point I'm trying to make here. What I'm saying is that in Blake's dark and twisted excuse for a brain, his reasoning makes sense. If he's not lying, maybe the other band members and I will be happy about what he has to say. (And please don't stop reading this book because you now think I'm too naive to root for. I know perfectly well that he could be lying.)

Am I babbling? I apologize. Look, I should probably lock myself in my bedroom and never speak to Blake again, but I'm going to take a major risk and play along one more time, okay? If it goes horribly wrong, you can shake your head in disappointment and say that you told me so.

I text Clarissa and Mel and ask if they can come over. They can, but they both need a ride. I tell Blake that I'm not willing to share a moving vehicle with him right now, which I assume will start another fight, but he says that he understands and that he'll be waiting when I get back. He doesn't say it in a spooky way: "I'll be here when you get back." I mean, that's what he says, but it's not foreboding. He'll just be home when we get back.

(I'm starting to feel like I should hire somebody to cowrite this book with me, just to help until I get my mind sorted out. This last page or so hasn't been my best work. But it has a raw honesty to it, right? Life, like punk rock, is messy.)

"How are things going with Audrey?" asks Mel as he gets in my car.

"She broke up with me."

Mel nods. "I heard you were writing poems for other girls."

"I was framed."

"I assumed so. Gretchen posted the poems online, and they're pretty awful. Everybody's making fun of them. Glad to hear it wasn't you."

"Let's save the talking until we get back to my house," I recommend.

I pick up Clarissa, who also wants to talk about Audrey and who will cover the merch table now that we're not dating. She suggests Blake. I reject this suggestion.

When we get back to my house, Blake has poured everyone a glass of cold, refreshing lemonade. Clarissa and Mel gratefully accept the beverages. I reluctantly take the glass, checking carefully for evidence that he spat in it. I don't see any froth at the top, so he probably didn't.

"I suppose you're wondering why I've called you here," says Blake.

"I thought Rod called us here," says Clarissa.

"No, it was me."

"Oh, I'm even more intrigued then."

(Warning: cliffhanger chapter ending approaching!)

Blake clears his throat. "I've called you here to…"

21.

LET YOU KNOW that I've booked three Fanged Grapefruit gigs for this weekend."

Clarissa and Mel look at each other.

"We can get our own gigs," I say.

"Not decent ones," says Blake. "You've been playing at the same dismal club for too long. We're going on a road trip."

"No, we're not," I inform him.

"Yes, we are," Blake corrects. "Friday night you're opening for Fist Knuckles."

Clarissa and Mel stare at each other again. Fist Knuckles is one of our top five musical influences. When we saw them live last year, the police had to turn a fire hose on them. (The band, not the audience.) It was a great show.

"No way," says Mel.

"Very much way," says Blake.

"No way," says Clarissa.

"Mucho way," says Blake.

"There's no way," I say.

"When Blake Montgomery manages your band, your band gets managed. And it's a paying gig."

"How much?" asks Mel, ignoring the horrifying part where Blake implied that he's now our manager.

Blake tells us. I'm not going to repeat the amount because I'm not sure what your expectations are for how much we'd get paid for opening for Fist Knuckles at a medium-sized club. The reality is probably less than what you're thinking, so I don't want the number to be a distraction. Let's just say that it's not really going to change our overall financial state but that it's an extremely fair amount. And it's more than paying for free.

"Sweet," says Mel.

"Saturday night, you're the middle act in a three-act bill of Don & the Keys, Fanged Grapefruit, and Krab Salad."

"Wait…Don & the Keys are opening for *us*?" asks Clarissa.

"Yes."

Clarissa and Mel exchange a high five. Don & the Keys (formerly the Donkeys) beat us in a talent show once, and they were obnoxious jerks about it. If they're opening for Fanged Grapefruit, their careers are going nowhere. Ha ha.

"Is Krab Salad spelled with a *K* or with a *C*?" asks Mel.

"With a *K*."

"I love them!"

"How much for that show?" asks Clarissa.

Blake tells us.

"Whoa," says Clarissa.

"I know, right?" says Blake.

I hate to be Mr. Dubious, but Blake is a long way from having earned my trust. "How do we know you aren't making this up?" I ask.

"You can check the websites," says Blake. "But don't do that yet because I haven't told you the best news. Sunday night, you're headlining."

"Headlining?" asks Mel. "Are you serious?"

"Completely serious."

"At a tiny, disgusting club?" asks Clarissa.

"Nope. It's not Madison Square Garden, but this place holds five hundred people."

"Where?" I ask, suspicious of Blake.

"Miami."

"We can't play in Miami on Sunday night. We have to go to school the next day."

"Only part of that is correct," says Blake.

"Are you saying we don't have to go to school Monday? Are you now so powerful that you can create a freak Florida snowstorm so schools are closed and we get the day off?"

"I wish. I'm getting us a tour bus for the weekend. We'll drive home each night. Sunday night, you guys will do the show and then get some sleep on the way back. We'll be back by 3:00 a.m. You'll be fine."

"A tour bus will cost more than we're making," I say.

"The bus is my treat to make up for my past behavior."

"Our parents will never go for this idea," I say.

"I can't speak for Mel's parents or Clarissa's parents because I've never had the pleasure of meeting them. But I'm pretty sure Aunt Connie will understand what a fantastic opportunity this is for you, and since you're not actually *skipping* school and you've been maintaining a high GPA and you haven't gotten into any trouble recently—at least not that the principal notified her about—I think she'll say yes."

"I think I could sell my mom and dad on it," says Mel.

"I think if I ask my dad first and let him plead my case to my mom, my parents will say it's okay as long as I promise to answer my phone even if my mom calls while we're onstage," says Clarissa.

"Perfect," says Blake. "It's Fanged Grapefruit's first tour!"

"You're not our manager," I tell him.

"Can I be your roadie?"

"No."

"I think he'd be fulfilling the duties of a roadie," says Mel.

"Do you two really want to succeed so badly that you'll let somebody as poisonous as Blake be involved in our future?"

"Pretty much, yeah," says Clarissa.

"We've had no luck setting up shows," says Mel. "Blake has only been here for a week, and he's managed to get us three good gigs. Clearly, he's doing something right."

"He's probably bribing them. Dude has too much disposable income."

"Look, I'm not trying to cause strife between the three of you," says Blake. "The only fair way to handle this is for you to put it to a vote."

"Sorry," I say, "but you don't get to decide if we put something to a vote. Only the founding members of Fanged Grapefruit get to decide if something goes to a vote."

"My mistake."

I don't want this to go to a vote because I know that Clarissa and Mel will vote in favor of playing these venues and I'll vote against it, and there will forever be the knowledge that I voted against three sweet gigs. I'll always be the band member who wasn't as committed to our success as the others.

"All in favor of taking these gigs, raise your hand," says Mel.

He raises his hand. Clarissa raises her hand. Though it

suddenly feels like it weighs fifteen hundred pounds, I raise my hand.

No way does this end well.

"Sure, you can do that," says Mom, robbing me of my chance to get out of this madness and blame a parent. "This can't become a weekly thing, but once in a while, of course."

"Thanks."

"It's good to see that you and Blake are finally getting along."

"Yep."

Mom narrows her eyes with concern. "You look upset. You should be happy. Is everything all right?"

"Audrey and I broke up."

"Oh no! What happened?"

"We drifted apart."

"Oh, Rod, I'm so sorry."

"It's okay."

"Do you need a banana split? I'll make you one."

"No, I'm fine."

The worst part of this arrangement is that I have to spend the next week pretending that I don't find Blake completely abhorrent. I speak to him as little as possible, but when we pass each other, I'm forced to nod politely. And we have to make conversation during meals. As Blake said approximately six thousand years ago, he's not a fan of small talk, so dinner conversation tends to focus on subjects like the national debt and the meaning of our existence. I think Mom is impressed.

Yes, he's in the garage every afternoon when we practice. And, yes, he makes suggestions. And, yes, Mel and Clarissa think his suggestions are oh-so-wonderful. And, yes, I will grudgingly admit that not all his suggestions are entirely worthless. But, no, I will not call him our manager.

Of course, I have to see Audrey every day in biology, and gosh, that's not awkward at all. It's also not the least bit awkward when I see Gretchen, Bernadette, Lorelei, Shannon, Melissa, and Jennifer. Nope, not at all. Jennifer does look like she feels guilty, though apparently not guilty enough to confess her role in Blake's plan.

I should be all bouncy and giddy over these upcoming shows, but how can I trust that Blake is really trying to help? How do I know he won't release a thousand sewer rats into the club as we take the stage? (Would that hurt our reputation or improve it? I'm not sure. Either way, I don't want to find out.) How do I know he didn't hack the venue websites to say we're playing? How do I know he won't purposely let the bus run out of gas so that we miss our show and damage our credibility?

I try to improve my mood with the realization that Blake has already been here for almost two weeks, which means that there are only two months and two weeks left to go! That's way better than having three months left. I have to take joy in the little things now.

Unrelated to Blake, what if Fanged Grapefruit isn't good enough to open for acts like Fist Knuckles and Krab Salad? What if we're booed off the stage? What if the audience stands there, bored? What if the club owner has to come out and apologize to everybody for letting them down by booking such a low-quality opening band? What if we finish our set and I look over to see the lead singer of Krab Salad shaking his head with disappointment? I'm not one to be plagued by self-doubt, but these all seem like realistic potential outcomes.

I force myself to be excited. This could be our big break! Blake coming to live with us could be the best thing that ever happened to me. The best thing ever! *Ever!* Yep, I'll keep telling myself that every six or seven minutes until my brain can't argue with me anymore and I believe it!

When I look at my bedroom, it no longer appears that his posters are gradually shifting over to my side, so that's something to celebrate, I guess.

For the record, his snoring doesn't get any quieter. And I really miss Audrey.

Hey, it's Friday afternoon already! Clarissa and Mel are at my house, and we keep making comments about how great these three shows are going to be. I have to admit that even though I'm leery of Blake's motives, I can't help but get excited. Fanged Grapefruit is more important to me than anything except Mom, food, and oxygen, so how can I *not* feel a little twitter in my tummy when the tour bus pulls up alongside my house?

Correction: the minivan.

"I thought it was going to be a bus," says Mel.

"It's like a bus," I say sarcastically. "Just a little smaller and not bus-shaped, and…y'know, a minivan."

Blake gets out of the passenger side. "Sorry it doesn't have your logo on the doors. They would've charged extra for the painting and repainting. What do you think?"

Remember how Blake was making snide remarks about my car after I picked him up at the airport? This minivan doesn't *quite* make him a hypocrite. (It's a perfectly fine vehicle, rust-free, a pleasant green color, and there's no evidence that any tires might pop off while we're driving.) But it's no tour bus.

"What happened to the bus?" I asked.

"I didn't say bus. I said van."

"Nope, you said tour bus. That's fine. I mean, it doesn't bother *me*. It looks like a nice sturdy soccer mom van. It's just not what our manager promised us."

"I'm pretty sure I said van."

I shake my head. "Again, nobody here is going to complain. We're a pretty easygoing group of people. It seemed worth mentioning that our mode of transportation has changed, but it's certainly not something that anybody is going to make a big deal about. You're not going to make a big deal about it, are you, Mel? Clarissa? We're all cool with a green van instead of a legit tour bus, right?"

"I thought he said bus too, but maybe I heard wrong," says Clarissa.

"Nah, you didn't hear wrong," I assure her. "I bet Fist Knuckles tours in a minivan too."

The driver of the minivan steps out of the vehicle.

If you were wandering along a desolate road after dark and this guy pulled up next to you, there's no way you'd get in his minivan. In fact, if he showed up in broad daylight and your car had broken down and you were on a busy street with dozens of witnesses, you'd still decline his offer for a ride. In fact, I'll go so far as to say that if you were at the grocery store and you saw this gentleman in one of the aisles, you'd decide to shop someplace else. Which is all to say, he's rather intimidating.

"Is there a problem?" the driver asks.

"No," I say.

"Good." The driver gets back in the minivan.

"I actually wasn't answering his question," I say. "That no was aimed at the idea of riding with him."

"What do you mean?" asks Blake.

"It's pretty simple, really. We're not getting in that minivan."

"For real? You guys are in a punk rock band, and you're scared of the guy's tattoos and scars and multicolored hair and metal teeth?"

"Those were all fine," I say. "It was his dead eyes."

"Sorry. I guess I forgot to request a driver that didn't have dead eyes."

"You're trying to be sarcastic, but I'm serious. I refuse to get murdered on our first out-of-town gig."

"I'm not sure I can get a refund," says Blake.

"Poor planning," I say.

"So you're canceling the tour?"

"Of course not. We'll take my car and have a cramped, miserable ride, thanks to our manager."

"If that's the way you want it."

"It's not. But for our safety, that's the way it has to be apparently."

Blake walks over to the minivan. Despite whatever impression you may have gotten, I don't wish for him to perish, so I carefully watch for signs that the driver may attempt to abduct or kill him. I'm not saying that I'll rush over there if I hear the roar of a chainsaw, but I'll shout a warning.

"You both agree with this, right?" I ask Clarissa and Mel.

"Oh, yeah," says Mel. "I wasn't going anywhere with the dead-eyed dude. I'm glad you said something."

The minivan drives off, leaving my cousin behind and alive.

"I tried to get us there in comfort," says Blake, shaking his head.

"And you failed," I say. "Everybody has to suck at something. Let's pack up my car."

One point for Team Rod. Heh, heh.

As we walk toward my car, I notice Blake grinning.

Why is he grinning?

Did I prematurely assign the point? Was this part of his plan too?

22.

THOUGH I'D BEEN happy that Blake messed up, I have to admit that I'm less merry about it now that we have a two-hour drive ahead of us. I was looking forward to letting somebody else worry about steering and accelerating and braking and stuff. I will still defend my car's honor, but it's not such a great mode of transportation when you've got four people and musical equipment packed in there. (Reminder: Clarissa is very tall.)

I was in favor of leaving Blake at home to think about what he'd done, but since he's the guy who set everything up, we pretty much had to bring him. But if he becomes too annoying, I won't hesitate to make him run alongside the vehicle.

There are a lot of madcap antics that can happen when a punk rock band drives an old car one hundred thirty-eight miles across Florida; however, the trip is not particularly wacky enough to detail for you, and we arrive at the venue ahead of schedule. The windows look like they're glowing blue, green, and pink, which is appropriate since the club is called Blue Green Pink Glow.

The four of us walk inside. Clarissa stops. "Do you smell that?"

"What?" I ask.

"Nothing. There's no scent. We've never played anywhere that doesn't have a distinctive odor."

"Look up at the ceiling," I say. "It's clean."

We all look up and admire the ceiling.

"Do you think it's been recently washed?" asks Mel. "Or did the stains not make it all the way up there?"

We walk over to the bar to introduce ourselves to the manager, marveling at the way our feet don't stick to the floor.

"That's the stage," says the manager, pointing to the elevated platform behind him. Obviously, we didn't need him to point it out, but this is the kind of venue where people are polite. "Get yourselves set up, and we'll do sound check in about thirty minutes. Can I get you guys anything to eat? Club sandwich? Nachos?"

Our first impulse is to decline his offer because none of us would dare consume any food from the Lane, not even a bag of chips from a vending machine. But here? I bet their club sandwiches contain the meats you'd typically associate with that type of sandwich instead of the Meat that Might Be Ham and/or Turkey, the Meat that Might Be Roast Beef and/or Bacon, and the Meat (?) that Could Be Anything. Put your guesses in the jar for a chance to win fifty bucks and food poisoning!

I bet their nachos wouldn't turn your digestive tract yellow.

I bet if I had a cherry cola, it wouldn't look like an oil slick, and the last sip wouldn't stretch from my mouth to the glass like cheese sticking to the pizza box.

So we have dinner. I'm not saying that it was Michelin star dining, but it's nice to be offered food that isn't actively harmful to our well-being.

We set up our instruments. Sound check goes perfectly.

The lead singer of Fist Knuckles (who also plays the piccolo in the most punk rock manner imaginable) walks up to the stage. "You Fanged Grapefruit?" he asks.

"Yes," I say. "We're big fans."

"Of Fanged Grapefruit?"

"No, of Fist Knuckles."

"That's cool. We're playing tonight."

"We know. We're opening for you."

"Interesting. Any idea where the stage is?"

"We're standing on it."

The lead singer looks down. "No, I'm not."

"We are. You're standing in front of it."

"If you don't know the answer to my question, you could simply say so."

"Sorry."

"Mind if I vomit?" he asks.

"Go right ahead. You're the headliner."

"Am I?"

"Yes, sir."

The lead singer smiles. "You bet your…"

We all wait for him to finish the thought.

"I can't remember what we were going to bet," he says.

"Our bottom dollar?" suggests Mel.

"You bet your bottom dollar I'm the headliner! Those other four losers in Fist Knuckles think they bring in the crowds, but it's all me, baby. It's all me. You'll tell them that, right?"

"Probably not," I admit.

"That makes sense."

The lead singer wanders off.

"I can't believe we get to open for Fist Knuckles!" says Clarissa, bouncing with excitement.

By showtime, the club is about half full, which means that it's by far the biggest audience we've ever performed for. I don't see any Fanged Grapefruit shirts out there, so Blake has been slacking on his bribes, but there's a definite energy in the crowd. As long as Blake doesn't sabotage the show, it's going to be incredible.

I'm sure he wouldn't sabotage it. He set up the gig.

I know what you're thinking. *Have you not been paying attention to your own book? Of course he'd sabotage the show, fool!*

But it would reflect badly on him too.

I know what you're thinking. *The mess-up with the mini-van also reflected badly on him, but that doesn't mean it wasn't a piece of his evil puzzle. He could* absolutely *be planning to sabotage the show, and if you're not prepared for that possibility, you're a simpleton.*

Still, maybe everything Blake did was to be more closely involved with Fanged Grapefruit. Maybe he's achieved his goal, and now it's in his best interest for everything to go well tonight.

I know what you're thinking. *Maybe you're right. Everything might go fine. However, as your reader, I want you to remain vigilant during the show. Don't let down your guard. Hope for the best and prepare for the worst, okay?*

Thanks. That sounds like a solid approach. I'll stay opti-mistic, but I won't be dumb about my optimism.

Mel, Clarissa, Blake, and I sit in the greenroom, which is—and I'm not exaggerating—eight trillion times better than the greenroom in the Lane. You can sit on this couch without wearing a hazmat suit. The bottles of water still have their original seal. At the Lane, they provide bottled water to the performers, but you can tell that they just filled the bottles with water from a faucet. The tint gives it away. And there are free apples. Apples! So healthy and delicious!

The door opens, and the owner sticks his head in. "Sixty seconds," he says.

Blake stands. "Good luck to all of you."

Wait. What did he mean by that?

I immediately do a mental replay of "Good luck to all of you." Was it sincere or menacing? His tone seemed to straddle the two options. He didn't wring his hands together and go "Muahahahahaha!" but I'm not convinced that he was genuinely wishing us good luck. Are we headed toward disaster? Should I warn Mel and Clarissa? Should I come up with some sort of excuse for me and Blake to walk outside of the club and then knock him unconscious and lock him in the trunk of my car so he can't follow through on his devious plan?

Hope for the best. Hope for the best. Hope for the best.

The owner takes the stage. "Thanks for coming out tonight," he says. "We've got a great show for you. Our headliner is the one, the only, the legendary, the angry, Fist Knuckles!"

The crowd goes berserk.

"But to start things off, please welcome Vampire Grapefruit!"

Close enough.

The crowd's level of berserkness (not a real word, but it should be) drops a bit, but we still get an enthusiastic greeting. Mel, Clarissa, and I walk on to the stage, and excitement shoots through me like electricity surging through Frankenstein's monster. I step up to the microphone.

"Thanks for coming to Blue Green Pink Glow! We're Fanged Grapefruit! Are you ready to *rock*?"

They sure are! No prepping needed for this crowd! They've arrived with every intention of rocking, and they're more than happy to answer my rhetorical question in the affirmative.

The audience is ready to rock. The band is ready to rock. Everybody is on the same page here. It's time to get this party started!

Good luck to all of you.

I wish I knew what Blake meant by that.

"All our songs tonight are originals," I tell the audience. "Have you ever tried to get a fish to catch popcorn in its mouth?"

I know perfectly well that they haven't, and they know that I know. But that doesn't stop the audience from cheering at the question. "Well, that's what this first song is about. It's called 'You Can't Train a Goldfish to Catch Popcorn in Its Mouth, So Don't Even Try.' *One, two, three, go!*"

We launch into the song, providing the audience with the raw material they needed to begin rocking. I've been to plenty of shows where the crowd treats the opening act as if they're purposely delaying everybody's fun, but not this crowd.

Good luck to all of you.

I glance around the club. I don't see any boxes that look like they could contain sewer rats.

I flub a chord, but I don't think anybody notices.

We're only on our first song, and the audience loves us! Oh, how Audrey would have loved this. She will regret breaking up with me! We'll be playing sold-out stadiums in London while she's still in biology class, identifying spleens.

Good luck to all of you.

I need to forget about Blake. There's simply no way he's going to try to ruin our show. If nothing else, he knows that we'd abandon him here. You don't sabotage somebody when they're your ride home.

I begin singing the third verse. Then I realize that I skipped the second verse. I wish I could say that it doesn't matter; however, these are story-driven lyrics, and I've left out a significant plot point. The arc of the fish and the feeder won't make sense now.

The audience is still rocking out, but I notice Clarissa giving me a funny look. It's okay. Punk rock is supposed to be rough around the edges, and only a few people were recording us with their cell phones.

The crowd's berserkity (This should also be a word.) increases as we do the big finish. Performance glitches aside, this is still the most receptive audience we've ever had.

"Thank you!" I say. "It's an honor to open for Fist Knuckles!"

The audience cheers at the name of the headliner. This is a common technique in the world of entertainment. If there is a more popular act playing later in the evening at the same venue, you mention them by name. This will cause the audience to react in a positive manner. Their response is goodwill toward the more popular act, but since *you're* onstage at the time, you're the recipient of the enthusiasm. It's win-win. If you go into the performing arts, I highly recommend this move.

We begin our second song.

Good luck to all of you.

Enough! I need to get Blake out of my head before I completely mess up my guitar playing like I just did.

We play our entire half-hour set. Here are some important details:

1. In terms of the size and enthusiasm of the crowd, it's the best show Fanged Grapefruit has ever done. And I don't think Blake bribed them, which makes it even more satisfying.

2. It is the best show Mel has ever played. His guitar playing is flawless. His energy level is amazing. His background vocals support my lead vocals in a way they've never been supported before.

3. It is the best show Clarissa has ever played. I've always been impressed by her drumming skills, but tonight it's like she's the human equivalent of an electronic drum machine. Actually, that's the worst possible description. She is raw and unplugged. Suffice it to say, she was awesome.

Before we move on to item #4, let's recap the first three.

1. Best Fanged Grapefruit show.
2. Best Mel show.
3. Best Clarissa show.

And now on to the fourth detail.

4. I mess up. A lot.

Does the audience notice? I don't think so. But Mel and Clarissa definitely notice. I fumble through some of my audience banter. I play quite a few wrong notes, and I screw up the lyrics on several occasions. I'm not saying that my performance was a complete disaster. Most of the time, my playing and singing were really good. But yeah, I play like it was like a practice session instead of a real show.

And, no, Blake didn't pull any stunts.

Unless you count making me so paranoid that he was going to sabotage the show that it impacted my music.

I'll count that.

23.

THE FOUR OF us sit in the greenroom after the show, eating apples.

"That was fantastic," says Blake.

"I want to move here," says Mel. "I want to drop out of school and play here every night." (Important note to students: Mel is kidding. Do not drop out of school.)

"Best show we've had yet," says Clarissa.

"Yep," I say.

Everybody crunches their bites of apple. The other four members of Fist Knuckles congratulated us on a job well done, which was one of the greatest honors of our lives. (At the time, the lead singer could not be found, though he was located a couple of blocks away and brought back in time for them to take the stage.) We can hear them playing now, and as soon as we finish our apples, we're going out to watch.

"So, Rod..." says Mel.

"Yes?"

"What happened?"

I shrug. "Nerves, I guess."

"You've never had nerves like that before."

"I know, but we've never had a crowd that size before."

"Well, the plan is for the crowds to get bigger and bigger."

"I apologize," I say. "That was a long way from my best per-formance. I let you guys down. I promise it won't happen again."

Mel seems satisfied with that answer. "Time for us to get used to success. Fanged Grapefruit is now on the map. Thanks, Blake!"

"Do you want me to ask the audience if they're ready to rock?" Mel inquires before we take the stage for our second gig of the weekend.

"No, I've got it."

"You sure?"

"I'm sure."

Club Marrow is about halfway between the Lane and Blue Green Pink Glow in terms of cleanliness. Your feet don't stick to the floor, but you'd put down a tablecloth before you ate off it. They gave us free nachos before the show, though the three of us had to share. The cheese-flavored sauce product was quite tasty.

The crowd is even bigger here, although I get the sense that we'll have to work harder for their affection. It's going to be a great show. Don & the Keys bombed, which will make this experience even greater because we are going to rock.

"Good luck to all of you," says Blake.

We take the stage.

Here's another helpful tip for those of you who may be considering a career in the musical arts: if you're obsessively focused on trying not to make mistakes, it can take some of the soul out of your performance. I screw up fewer times than I did last night (though I still screw up), but though I hit more of the correct notes, my singing and guitar playing don't have my usual passion.

Mel and Clarissa are in top form again, and they help balance things out. But still, it's a below-average show for Fanged Grapefruit. The audience likes us, but they don't love us. Nobody is particularly disappointed when I announce that we're on our last song. A couple of people in the audience are clearly playing games on their phones, and when we depart the stage, I know that nobody is going to drive home saying, "I was all excited for Krab Salad, but much to my surprise, one of their opening acts blew them away! Fanged Grapefruit rules! Wooooooo!"

Nobody says much of anything as we break down our equipment and load it into my car. When we're done, we sit quietly in the greenroom, which does not have apples.

"Hmm," says Blake.

"I thought that went okay," says Mel.

"Yeah," says Clarissa.

"It was a pretty good show," I confirm.

Clarissa turns to face me. "We can say that because we're trying to make you feel better, but you're not allowed to agree with us."

"What was wrong with it?" I ask. When deciding how to handle an uncomfortable situation, it's rare that I select the "play stupid" option, but that's what I do this time.

"You weren't any good," says Clarissa. "You were generic."

I expected her to say something like *terrible, awful, disgraceful, wretched, dismal,* or *horrendous.* I never imagined that she would be so hurtful as to use the G-word.

"Generic?" I repeat. "What do you mean?"

"You weren't connecting with the audience. You weren't Rod Conklin. You were some guy with a decent voice who knows how to play a guitar."

"Do you agree with her?" I ask Mel.

Why did I ask that question? Of course he agrees with her! She's absolutely right! Now I've forced him to say it out loud! What's the matter with me?

"Yeah, I agree," says Mel. "You did okay with the technical stuff, but your performance was kind of hollow."

Hollow. Generic. If I had to list all the words that I would *not* want to appear on my tombstone, those would be in the top ten.

"Look, it wasn't my best show," I admit, "but you're both being harsh."

"No, we're not," says Clarissa. "We're being gentle. We whispered the harsh stuff to each other while we were loading my drums."

"I can't help but feel personally responsible for this," says Blake. "I'm the one who got you these higher profile gigs, and I didn't consider the extra pressure it would put on all of you. It was unfair of me to do that to Rod, and I apologize."

"I can handle pressure," I insist.

"Of course you can," says Blake. "And I agree with you. Mel and Clarissa are maybe being a smidgen too harsh. As the lead singer, if you fail, the band fails, so you're under even more pressure than everybody else. In your position, maybe Mel would've cracked too."

"I didn't *fail*," I say. "And I didn't crack."

"I never said you did," says Blake. "Nobody said you did. Or if they did, they didn't say it to me. If they had, I would've disagreed with them. I'm on your side, Rod. Sometimes we simply don't deliver. What's important isn't whether or not you let your bandmates down but whether you recognize what happened and apologize."

"Can you excuse us for a minute, Blake?" asks Clarissa.

"Certainly." He stands and walks over to the door of the greenroom. "I'll be right outside if you need me." He leaves.

"We thought this conversation should be private between the band members," says Mel.

Suddenly, every part of my body itches. I resist the urge to start vigorously scratching.

"We appreciate that your cousin gave us these opportunities," says Clarissa. "But we really need you to step up your game. This can't happen again. Tomorrow we're the main act. We can't mess this up."

"Or else what?" I ask.

"There's no 'or else.' We're not making threats. We're only asking you to do better next time."

"I will," I promise. "You have my word. This was my last soulless show."

Everybody falls asleep on the drive home—well, all except for me. I'm the one driving. And I'm too worried that Blake's snoring is going to put the tires out of alignment to doze off. I have no idea how Mel and Clarissa can sleep through that. Then I wonder if they're pretending to be asleep so they don't have to talk to me.

Miami. The club is a lot smaller than we expected (No way does this hold five hundred people, unless they're all wearing mandatory corsets.), but it's still bigger than the Lane. It's probably better that the venue is small. Less empty space if we don't pack 'em in.

Our opening act consists of three high school freshmen who pretend to be playing instruments but are actually strumming along to background tracks they're playing through their phone. They're singing for real though. We know this because if the vocals were recorded, they definitely would have done another take.

"At least we won't have any trouble competing with that," I say to Mel and Clarissa as we watch offstage.

"We're not trying to compete," says Clarissa. "We're trying to be the best Fanged Grapefruit we can be."

I knew that.

As the opening act announces that they're on their last

song, Blake asks if he can talk to me for a minute. We walk to a private corner.

"You're not going to mess this up for me, right?" he asks.

"Excuse me?"

"You made me look bad the past two shows. I put my neck out for you, Rod. These venues expect one hundred percent commitment, and the last two places only got two-thirds of that."

"Are you questioning my commitment?"

"No, but Mel and Clarissa are."

"They may be questioning my ability to handle stress, but they're *not* questioning my commitment. Nobody is more committed to Fanged Grapefruit than me. Nobody."

"All right, all right. But you do realize that you weren't awesome Friday or Saturday night, correct?"

"It's already been discussed. We don't need to revisit it."

"I understand. But again, these gigs weren't easy to set up. I promised a certain quality of product, and I need you to deliver."

I clench my fists. "And I'm sure it's a coincidence that you're bringing it up now, minutes before we go onstage?"

"When else would I bring it up?"

"Anytime in the past twenty-four hours would've been better. I know what you're doing, Blake. You're trying to make me choke."

"Why would I want that?"

"Because you're trying to ruin my life."

Blake laughs. "If I wanted to ruin your life, I wouldn't set up amazing gigs for your band."

"I disagree."

"Seems like a lot of work. There have to be easier ways to ruin somebody's life."

"Don't talk to me anymore."

"Okay, Rod, I can see that I've upset you, and that wasn't my intention. You'll be great tonight. You won't play any wrong notes, and you won't accidentally switch around any lyrics. And your stage presence will be better than a robot. I have faith in you, cousin. You'll totally redeem yourself."

"This isn't going to work," I tell him. "It's obvious what you're trying to do, so your negativity can't have any impact."

"Good. I'm glad it can't have any impact. Because the last thing I want is for you to go out onto that stage and do poorly. I'd never want to see a situation where Clarissa and Mel have to question your future with the band."

"You're still trying to sabotage me, and you're still being obvious about it."

"All I'm saying is that sometimes we squander the opportunities we've been given, and it haunts us for the remainder of our days. Clarissa and Mel don't need it, but good luck to you."

Fanged Grapefruit takes the stage. The lights seem brighter. They kind of hurt my eyes, but I don't stop the show to whine about it.

"Thanks for coming out tonight! We're Fanged Grapefruit! Are you ready to *rock*?"

The audience cheers.

Oh, by the way, it was Mel who said that, not me. Yeah, I know. I'm not happy about it either. He offered again, so I accepted through gritted teeth.

I'm ashamed to admit that I secretly hope he'll mess it up ("Are you ready to *tap dance*?") so that the fingers of blame won't all point at me if the show goes badly. But he does fine. If I was in the audience and I heard his yes/no question, I'd answer yes.

Blake's mind games worked on me the first time, and they worked on me the second time too. But they are *not* going to work on me a third time! I know what he's doing. I'm immune.

Good luck to you.

See? That sentence, even in italics, doesn't stress me out anymore. His attempt to psyche me out is laughable. Totally laughable. I'd laugh out loud about it right there onstage, but, no, that's something a crazy person would do.

Good luck to you.

Yes, his words are playing through my mind on an endless loop, but that doesn't mean they're having an effect.

He threw me off because I was sure that he had plans to sabotage the show. Now that I know he doesn't, I can ignore him and focus on…

What if he didn't sabotage the first two shows so that I wouldn't be prepared for the third? What if tonight's the night he releases the rats?

There was no room in my car for a box of rats.

What if he had the box of rats delivered directly to the venue?

What if his sabotage isn't related to rats?

He could do anything.

Anything.

No, he's not going to disrupt the show. He played his silly little mind games before I stepped out into the way-too-bright lights that are hurting my eyes and making me a little dizzy, but that's as far as he'll take it.

I glance up at the ceiling. There are no buckets up there that might contain foul substances for him to drop upon the band or the audience during the show.

Am I succumbing to paranoia? Has Blake won yet another round?

What if I pretend to pass out? They can't hold it against

me if I collapse. They'd be heartless monsters if they got mad at me for losing consciousness onstage.

No, I probably shouldn't do that. I should make sure this is the best show of all time.

I realize that Mel and Clarissa are staring at me. Oh, yeah, I'm supposed to be singing and playing now. My bad.

You lose, Mr. Blake Montgomery. This show is going to be *phenomenal.*

24.

WE'RE DRIVING HOME.

Clarissa is in the passenger seat up front because she needs the most leg room. Mel is behind her. Blake is behind me. Sure, why shouldn't I have a monster behind me, staring at the back of my head while I try to concentrate on driving?

I suppose you're wondering how the show went. Let's just say that there were parts of it that went well and that there were parts of it that didn't go quite so well. As an example of a part of the show that went well, I'll direct you to Clarissa's drumming. She did a superb job. You won't hear any complaints from anybody about that. If you came to the show exclusively to hear Clarissa drumming, by golly, you got your money's worth.

Now if we switch gears and discuss the parts of the show that went less well than Clarissa's drumming, I guess we should touch upon the lackluster performance of Mel during the bridge of "I Shouldn't Have Had That Sixteenth Energy

Drink." Not his best guitar playing by any stretch of the imagination. He was a little off-key. He was out of synch with the drums, and his vocals were—let's be honest—subpar.

I'm not sure why Mel flubbed that part. He's usually extremely professional. If I had to guess, I'd say that he was slightly distracted by the fact that I had completely screwed up that song.

Oh, yeah, another element of the show that didn't go so well was me. It's my book, and I can make up anything I want. But a lot of people whipped out their cell phones when I started to mess up, and the videos are out there for the world to ridicule. I don't know what happened. Yes, I was exhausted. Yes, I was hyper-focused on trying not to make a mistake while at the same time keeping vigilant for Blake's sabotage. Yes, I had a moment in the second song when it suddenly hit me that Audrey had broken up with me and I felt sad and alone. Yes, I kept hearing Blake's voice in my head, and I kept seeing little floating transparent Blake-heads, and...actually, I guess all these elements, put together, explain pretty clearly why my performance was so wretched.

If I'd done this badly the first time Mel or Clarissa heard me play, there never would have been a Fanged Grapefruit. The interaction would've gone like this:

[I play and sing.]

ROD: Wanna form a band?

MEL/CLARISSA: Oh, goodness, no!

At least the manager of the club paid us. Oh, wait. He didn't. He explained to Blake that he'd taken a chance on an untested band like Fanged Grapefruit, and now many of the club's patrons who'd been there tonight would choose other venues when they were in the mood for musical entertainment. We were welcome to try to sue him for our fee. But if we did, he'd play a recording of our performance for the judge, and the judge would issue an order forbidding us from ever playing music again. We knew that the courts didn't really have the authority to end our musical careers, but we also knew that we weren't getting our cash.

Anyway, we're driving home, and as you might expect, it's a bit awkward.

Finally, Blake speaks. "So who wants to go first?"

"I don't want to hear anything from you," I tell him. "Not one single word out of your mouth. My car, my rules."

"We can't keep our heads in the sand."

"I can shove *your* head in the sand if you don't stop talking. I'll do a Google search for the nearest patch of quicksand. Don't think I won't."

"Very well."

"This is all your fault."

"You're right," says Blake. "I played horribly tonight."

"You know what I mean."

"I never set foot on the stage. I didn't say a word during the show. In fact, I left halfway through because it was too painful to witness."

I remember that moment clearly because when Blake walked away, I thought that it must be when he was preparing to strike. He didn't. Or maybe he was ready to but simply decided that I was doing such a good job of sabotaging myself that further efforts were not necessary on his part.

I want to bellow, "This is your fault! Your fault! Your fault!" over and over at him, but no matter how many times I shout this, it will be difficult to make the case with my bandmates. And I have to admit that I should've been less susceptible. If Blake was able to undermine my self-confidence like that, maybe I'm not cut out for the life of a professional musician. Maybe I should start shopping for ties for the office job I'll have after college. Trade in my lyrics for spreadsheets. Practice saying, "TGIF," by the water cooler.

Uh-oh, is there a tear trickling down my cheek? Please don't let Clarissa glance over and see it. Should I wipe it off, or will that draw more attention to it?

"You don't have to cry," says Blake, who can apparently see my tear-stained face in the rearview mirror.

"I'm not crying," I say.

"Leave him alone, Blake," says Clarissa. "He can cry if he wants to."

"I'm not crying," I say.

"I can see the tear," says Clarissa, "but that's okay. I'd probably be crying too."

"At least he didn't cry onstage," says Blake. "That's one positive thing we can take from this experience. The show would've been way worse if he'd started bawling. I hope we never have to find out how that would look."

"I'm serious, Blake," I say. "I will track down some quicksand."

"I apologize," says Blake. "You won't hear another word from me. It's all my fault for setting up big shows before you were ready. I should have gauged it better."

"That was fifteen more words," I say.

"It was more than fifteen. No wonder you can't keep time. You can't count."

"Blake, I asked you to leave him alone," says Clarissa. "One more word, and you're riding as a hood ornament."

Blake nods.

"Rod," says Clarissa, and I can tell from the way she says

my name that this is going to be a very serious conversation that I'm not going to enjoy. "Mel and I have been talking."

"When?"

"When you went to the restroom after the show."

"So what...I can't go to the restroom anymore without you talking about me?"

"You're already missing the point."

"What is the point?" I ask.

Mel leans forward, at least as much as he can because he is wearing a seat belt. "For starters, we're no longer going to accept any help from Blake."

Did I hear that correctly? Are they severing ties with Blake instead of me? Did they realize that this whole nightmare is his fault?

"Huh?" says Blake. I don't mind that he said another word. He can say, "Huh?" as often as he wants.

"It wouldn't be fair," says Mel. "He's your cousin, and we can't in good conscience let him continue to find us gigs, all things considered."

"What things considered? What are the things?"

Mel and Clarissa both sigh.

"Are you kicking me out of Fanged Grapefruit?" I ask.

"We were thinking more that the band should take a break," says Clarissa.

"A break? A gosh-darn, flipping break?" (I do not say "gosh-darn" or "flipping." I'll let you substitute other adjectives as you please.) "You guys can't kick me out of the band! Where's my due process? There's no Fanged Grapefruit charter that gives you the right to get rid of me! No! I won't go!"

"It's a majority vote," says Clarissa.

"Well, I vote against it."

"Yeah, okay, we figured that you would, but it's still two to one."

I violently shake my head. "I don't accept this! We created Fanged Grapefruit together! We practice in my garage! I wrote the best verse of the fish and popcorn song! You do *not* get to kick me out! I refuse to leave!"

"We thought you might feel this way," says Mel quietly. "If that's the way you're going to act, we can't kick you out. So Clarissa and I are officially quitting Fanged Grapefruit."

"You can't quit on Clarissa's behalf!"

"I quit," says Clarissa.

"Oh, really? You quit, huh? What are you going to do? Form your own band?"

"Yes," says Mel.

"It'd better not be called Fanged Grapefruit!"

"It won't."

"It'd better not be called anything like Fanged Grapefruit! It'd better not have any references to teeth or fruit!"

"We can't promise that," says Clarissa.

"And you'd better not use any of the other names that we rejected! I've got a list! I'll know!" I bellow over the rumble of the engine.

"We don't like any of those names," says Mel.

"And you can't play punk rock!"

"Of course we can play punk rock," says Clarissa.

"Well, you can't play any of the songs I wrote! Those are my intellectual property!"

"Everybody contributed to every song we play," says Mel.

"Then nobody gets to play any of them!"

"Why not divide them up?" suggests Blake.

"I didn't give you permission to speak again," Clarissa tells him. "This is between us."

"I want you both to pay your share of the rent from the time we spent practicing in my garage," I say, though I'm aware that this may be an unreasonable demand. "And it's time you started chipping in for gas."

"We chip in for gas all the time," says Mel.

He's right. They do. Clarissa paid for the fuel we're using at this very moment. "No, you don't," I say because I'm not in the mood for truth.

"We understand that you're upset," says Mel. "But I hope you understand our decision."

"I don't. You both suck."

"Fair enough."

"Kick me out of the band if you want," I say, "but I call the right to burn all the Fanged Grapefruit merchandise."

"You can burn it," says Mel, "but you can't record the fire and post the video online."

"Yes, I can. That would be the whole point of doing it."

"No. We don't accept those terms."

"Fine," I say. "I'll burn it for my own pleasure."

"We're okay with that."

"I'm not," says Clarissa. "Someday we'll wish we still had those stickers and shirts. You can burn your third of the merchandise, but I'm keeping my third."

"Actually, yeah, I'm keeping my third too," says Mel.

"You're not allowed to profit from it," I say.

"We don't want to profit from it," says Clarissa. Or Mel. Does it even matter at this point which one of them is speaking? "We want to keep the stuff as souvenirs."

"Souvenirs of the time you stomped on my heart!" I proclaim. "So if you're ever sitting around thinking that you're a good person, you can look down at your Fanged Grapefruit T-shirt and see that you're not!"

No! Another tear is forming! I try to blink it away before it gains momentum, but I think it's too late. The tear rolls down my cheek.

I glance over to see if Clarissa's noticed, and a tear rolls down Clarissa's cheek.

It's hard to tell because it's dark out and I'm looking at his face in the rearview mirror, but I think a tear rolls down Mel's cheek as well.

Yep, we're three punk rock musicians, weeping. How charming.

I have no girlfriend, and I have no band. He did it. I don't want to be melodramatic, but Blake has successfully ruined my life.

25.

I SORT OF wish that Mel and Clarissa had waited a few hours to kick me out of the band. We've still got a long drive together, and it's going to be ridiculously uncomfortable. Maybe they were worried that I'd kick them out of the car. Or maybe they were worried that I'd accuse them of waiting until we got home to do their dirty work just so I wouldn't kick them out of the car.

My prediction is right though. The drive home is ridiculously uncomfortable. It's late, and we have school tomorrow. I'm sure that Mel and Clarissa would like to get some sleep, but they both stare out the window. Maybe they feel too guilty about sleeping while I'm driving. Or maybe they don't dare sleep in a car with an angry driver. I don't know. We're no longer bandmates or friends, so I'm done trying to figure out their motives. Who cares?

Blake falls asleep just fine. And he begins snoring.

"Poke him," I tell Mel. "He doesn't get to snore in my car anymore."

Mel jabs Blake in the side. Blake pops awake. "What?"

"You were snoring."

"I don't snore."

"Then you were talking in your sleep in a foreign language that sounds like snoring."

Blake closes his eyes. "I'll try to be quieter."

"No, you'll stay awake," I say.

"Why?"

"Because if I drift into the opposite lane, I'll need you to shout a warning."

"Can't Mel or Clarissa do it?"

"I'm telling you to do it."

"All right, all right." Blake opens his eyes. "You're mad because everything you've worked for is gone."

"Maybe there was some confusion," I say. "Your talking privileges are still revoked. If I don't drift into the other lane, I don't want to hear anything from you."

"But—"

"Mouth closed."

Blake doesn't say another word. Neither does anybody else. Every time I peek at him in the rearview mirror, Blake looks very pleased with himself. I kind of wish I'd let him sleep.

We arrive at Clarissa's house. I want to say, "Unload your *own* drums, hag!" but that would be needlessly impolite. She gives me a hug when we're done, but I don't return it. I let my arms dangle.

When I drop off Mel, he mutters, "See you at school tomorrow." I want to say, "Not if I see you first!" but that's weak and too jovial. I could also point out that it's *already* tomorrow and that I'll see him at school *today*, idiot, but that also doesn't reach the level of devastating wit that I require. Instead I settle for says, "Kay."

Blake leans forward. "I'm not sure if you want me to stay in the back so you don't have to be near me or if you want me to move up to the front seat so you don't look like my chauffeur."

"I don't care where you sit."

"I'll stay in the back then."

"No. Sit up front. I'm not your limo driver."

(I'll admit it. Whatever choice Blake made, I'd have demanded that he do the other one.)

Blake climbs into the front seat. "I hope we're not mortal enemies."

"Oh, we are *so* mortal enemies. Remember how I used to pretend to tolerate you? Those days are over. From now on I will only look at you with disgust."

"Then these next four months aren't going to be very pleasant for either of us."

"Four? What do you mean four?"

"Haven't you heard?"

"No. What? What? What?"

"My parents have extended their cruise."

"*What?*"

Blake grins. "Just kidding."

"You don't get to joke around with me! We're enemies! Enemies don't have playful banter!"

"My mistake."

Mel walks out of his house and over to the car. "Is something wrong?" he asks. "I looked through the window and saw that you were still here, so I wanted to make sure that everything's okay."

"It's fine. Go back inside and start thinking up new band names." I back my car out of his driveway and go home.

Any day at school in which you literally get no sleep the night before is going to be a rough one. But word of the destruction of my band has traveled fast. This is, of course, not long after word traveled fast about my breakup with Audrey.

If it was only the Audrey thing, there could almost be a silver lining. *Sorry to hear you broke up with Audrey. So you're single now, huh? I heard your show at the Lane went really well.* But when you get kicked out of your own band for incompetence, that silver lining goes bye-bye.

Not that anybody flirted with me last week. Maybe the ladies were waiting a respectable amount of time before they pounced.

I fail a history quiz. No, the teacher doesn't grade it on the spot, but when you leave half of the answers blank, it's not a good sign.

In gym I'm not paying attention, and I take a volleyball to the head. It's not as bad as a baseball or a bowling ball, but it's enough to knock me off my feet. Enough to make me kind of woozy. I refuse an offer to go to the nurse because I've been the subject of too much discussion already. I don't want kids laughing about how I had to go to the nurse because I got bonked on the head by a volleyball.

In biology I'm so intent on ignoring Audrey that I spill a full dissection tray on my pants. (Despite the misery of my life right now, I want to be fair and make it clear that we do more in this class than just slice up dead organisms. The timing is purely coincidental.)

As I step out into the hallway after the final bell, Blake is standing nearby with a group of friends. They're all smiling and laughing as if they don't have a care in the world. Oh, look. One of them just high-fived Blake. It's really super that he has such close friends, isn't it?

I stand at my locker. I finally decide that I'm never going to get my combination right, so I give up.

"You're at the wrong locker," says Audrey, walking up to me.

I move one locker to the left. I'm not going to thank her.

"Sorry about your band," she says.

"No, you're not."

"Of course I am."

I really don't want her sympathy right now. What I want is for her to say is, *Will you take me back?* so that I can say, *No! Ha!* but that's unlikely. First, because she's not going to take me back, and second, because if she did, I'd definitely say yes.

"I honestly don't care if you're sorry about my band or not," I say. "If you want to clear your conscience, clear it someplace else."

Okay, this combination lock isn't opening either. But hey, if my fingers can't play guitar anymore, why should they be able to spin a tiny dial to the correct numbers?

I want Audrey to leave before she says something like, *Oh, by the way, I've met another guy. He's the most amazing human being ever. He's in a ska band, and he can dissect a squid while wearing a blindfold.* Or before she tells me that she's dating Blake.

No…

She wouldn't dare…

My mouth blurts out the question before my brain has fully processed the implications. "Are you going out with Blake?"

"I beg your pardon?"

"My cousin Blake."

"I knew which Blake you meant."

"Is he your new boyfriend?"

"Did you really just ask me that?"

"Is that a no?"

"Do you seriously think I'd go out with Blake?"

"No, but I'd feel better if you denied it."

"I'm not going out with Blake. I can't believe you even asked me that. You're losing your mind, Rod." Audrey storms off.

Yes, I feel stupid for having asked, but at least she isn't going out with Blake. I try the lock a few more times, decide that I'm not likely to get any homework done anyway, and give up.

I stumble a bit as I walk down the hallway toward the school exit. If I see anybody holding a grapefruit, I know I'll totally lose it, but nobody has one, at least not that they show me. It's possible that any citrus product could've set me off, so I'm glad we didn't have to find out for sure.

I walk out to the parking lot, where Blake is waiting by my car. I'm done being surprised by his sheer nerve.

Mom was asleep when we got home, and I didn't wake her up before I left for school, so she doesn't know that Fanged Grapefruit is history. She'd texted me to ask how it went, and I texted back that it went Great! with a promise of I'll tell you all about it tonight! Now I text her again:

Lots of practice to do. Can I stay over at Mel's?

She texts back a moment later. On a school night?

We'll study. I promise.

I wanted to hear about your show.

You will.

Blake will give spoilers!

He'll be at Mel's too. We've got a ton of stuff to work out. Please?

sigh Yes, but remember that school has to come before music.

Thanks, Mom!!!

I stick my cell phone back into my pocket as I reach the car. Blake gets into the passenger seat as if nothing's wrong. "How was your day?" he asks.

"Unspeakably horrific, thanks for asking."

He waits until I've driven away from school before speaking again. "You know I did you a favor, right?"

"Pretty sure you didn't."

"Mel and Clarissa were holding you back."

"Yes, that's why you planted seeds of doubt in my mind to freak me out. You wanted me to reach my full musical potential."

"Is that so hard to believe?"

"Yep."

He sighs. "If you don't want to recognize when people are doing you favors, that's your right."

"It sure is."

"You missed the turn," Blake points out.

"Hmm."

Blake frowns. "You're looking a little crazy-eyed, Rod. I'm no fan of driving, but maybe I should take over."

"Request denied."

"Where are we going?"

"It's a magical surprise."

"I've got homework."

"Me too."

"Are you going to kill me and dump my body somewhere?" Blake asks. He gives a nervous chuckle that indicates he was ninety-eight percent kidding, but he's focused on the remaining two percent of doubt.

"Nope."

"You sure?"

"Yep. Not gonna kill you."

"Then what are you doing?"

"I'm driving you back to California."

26.

NO, YOU'RE NOT," says Blake.

"I sure as heck am."

"Do you know how far it is from Florida to California?"

"I sure as heck do."

"Twenty-five hundred miles."

I nod. "Your calculation is correct."

"That's two thousand, five hundred miles."

"Yep."

"You really think you're going to drive me back to California and then get back in time for school tomorrow?"

"No, Blake," I say. "I do not believe that my car is capable of defying the laws of time and space."

"So…"

"So?"

"So…what? We're going on a three-day truancy road trip?"

"*Now* you've got it!"

"Aunt Connie will freak."

"I told her we're spending the night at Mel's."

"What are you going to do when school calls her tomorrow and says that we have unexcused absences?"

"I'll figure it out then."

"I don't think you planned this very well," says Blake.

"Maybe not."

Blake reaches into his pocket. I push the switch to make the automatic window go down. When he pulls out his cell phone, I grab it out of his hand and fling it out of the car.

"Hey!" he shouts. "What do you think you're doing?"

"I can't have you calling the police."

"I wasn't going to call the police! I was going to call your mom!"

"Can't have that either."

"You probably cracked the screen!"

"Then you shouldn't have taken it out of your pocket when I was rolling down the window. What did you think I was going to do? Use your brain, Blake!"

"I didn't think you'd destroy valuable property!"

"Then you miscalculated how angry I am. You said I had crazy eyes. Maybe in the future you'll know not to take out your cell phone when a crazy-eyed driver is rolling down the window."

"You've proven your point. Let's go back and get it."

"Nope."

"I'm not riding all the way to California without any games."

"We'll play 'I Spy with My Little Eyes' if we get bored."

"You're paying for that phone."

"Have your people send an invoice to my people."

"C'mon, Rod, this is ridiculous. Are you seriously kidnapping me?"

"Depends on how you define kidnapping."

"Driving me across the country against my will."

"Oh, then yeah, I'm definitely kidnapping you. Totally."

"What do you think is going to happen?"

"I'll drop you off at your house, and you'll stay there."

"There are a million logic errors with that."

"I agree," I say. "Your problem is that you're treating this like it was a carefully thought out scheme rather than me being spontaneous."

"Very well. If I'm being kidnapped, I guess there's nothing I can do." He reclines the seat. "I'm taking a nap. Let me know when we get there."

Blake closes his eyes.

A few minutes later I pull onto the highway.

A few minutes after that, Blake opens his eyes.

"Can't sleep?" I ask.

"This joke has gone far enough," he says.

"If it were a joke, I'd agree with you."

"You could end up in jail."

"You'll visit me, right?"

"You're going too fast."

"I think I'm going the perfect speed."

"Rod, I mean it. You're going too fast."

"How fast would you like me to go?"

"The speed limit."

"Speed limits are for boring people," I say.

I should clarify something about my mental state right now. I'm nowhere near as sane as I was at the beginning of this book, but I'm not quite as insane as I want Blake to believe. I'm crazy enough to kidnap my cousin, but not crazy enough to rev my car to one hundred and ten miles per hour and ram it into the concrete median. (Not that my car could go that fast without falling apart anyway.) So to summarize, yes, I'm faking. But, yes, Blake is right to be worried. But I'm only going five miles an hour over the state speed limit, and I'm using my turn signal and looking before I change lanes.

"All right, it's obvious that you're very, very tired," says Blake. "It's understandable. You drove all night. Maybe you should get some rest, and then we can revisit this whole road trip idea when you're refreshed."

I do a sudden swerve that makes Blake yelp.

"Sorry," I said. "Thought I saw a goat in the road."

"There are no goats on the highway!"

"A yak then."

"You're gonna get us killed!"

"Nahhhhhh. That doesn't sound like me."

"I apologize, okay?" says Blake. "I apologize for everything! It was wrong, and I admit it."

"What are you apologizing for exactly?"

"I said! Everything!"

"I'd like some specifics."

"Pull off at the next exit and I'll give you all the specifics you want!"

"I don't think so, Mr. Blakey-Poo," I say. "You'll tell me what I want to hear, and then I'll still be stuck with you for two more months. Much better to take you back to California."

"But that's ludicrous!"

"That's why it'll be so much fun!"

I guess I didn't tell you if I'm legitimately planning to drive Blake all two thousand five hundred miles back to his home or if this is a prank. The answer is that I'm serious.

I know, I know, I know. That's not the kind of behavior you expect from the heroes of books you read. But Blake left me no choice! What else am I supposed to do? If I don't get rid of my cousin soon, I'll be so far gone that this whole book will be another six hundred pages of me thinking, *Blah blah rrraar blah snorkle giggle blah blah woooo.*

Blake lets out a deep sigh. "I know why you're doing this. You want to hear me beg."

"Nope," I say, although I'm not going to lie. Hearing him beg would be pleasant.

"Well, I'm not going to give you the satisfaction. I'm not going to say another word for the rest of the trip."

"I love that idea. Challenge accepted."

And so we drive in silence.

After about twenty minutes, I start to consider that I've had better ideas in my life than abducting my cousin. What am I doing? I can't miss school tomorrow because of this! I have to turn back! I need to ask my history teacher for an extra credit assignment to make up for the quiz I bombed today!

And yet...if I give up, Blake will have the upper hand pretty much forever.

He could do even worse stuff. He could make me get straight Fs in school and ruin my college potential. He could burn down my house. He could make my life so miserable that I'll want to devote my entire existence to trying to unlock the secret of time travel in order to go back to prevent my own birth.

Really, I doubt he'd actually burn down my house. He's more subtle than that. But I absolutely can*not* let him win this round. And if I have to drive him all the way across the United States of America to add a point to my (currently empty) score column, I'll do it.

I keep driving.

We hit the hour mark. Blake remains silent. He's staring out the window like a droid in hibernation mode.

Two hours.

Two hours and eleven minutes.

Two hours and nineteen minutes.

Two hours and twenty-six minutes.

"You're low on gas," says Blake.

"Ha!" I shout. "You spoke! I won the battle of wills! Loser! Loser! *Loser!*"

"That's fine, but we're still running out of gas."

"Admit that I won! I want to hear you say it! 'Rod, you won.' Say it! Why won't you say it? Speak the words, Blake! Speak 'em!"

You know what? Maybe I'm even less grounded than I thought. I didn't expect to have quite that big of an outburst when Blake finally spoke. And the hysterical giggling doesn't help. I'll be honest. Blake isn't safe in this car with me.

He looks scared.

"Yeah, we'll stop for gas," I say.

"Thank you."

That fool. If he'd let us run out of gasoline, we would've been stuck by the side of the highway, and he would've been saved! I guess Blake Montgomery isn't so perfect, now is he?

I pull off at the next exit.

"Are you going to make a run for it when I stop at the pump?" I ask.

Blake shakes his head. "No."

"Are you sure?"

"You'd shoot me in the back."

"Oh, I don't have a weapon," I tell him. I want him to be intimidated by me, but there have to be boundaries.

"Still, I'm not going to try to escape."

"How do I know you're telling the truth?"

"Because you'll stop at the pump and I won't leave."

"That sounds suspicious."

"Did you bring handcuffs?"

"No, sorry."

"Do you want to lock me in the trunk?"

"Yeah, but I don't want somebody to see me doing it."

"Then maybe you should have worked out a plan for refueling the car before you dragged me along."

"I said this was spur of the moment."

"Still, you knew that your car didn't get twenty-five hundred miles to the gallon, right?"

"Yes."

"I'm surprised it gets four miles to the gallon."

"Now is not the time to criticize my car."

I pull into the gas station and stop in front of a pump. If Blake unfastens his seat belt, I'll instruct him in a very firm tone to immediately refasten it. If he unfastens his seat belt and opens the door, I'll try to kick it closed before he gets out. If he unfastens his seat belt, opens the door, and gets out...well, I don't know if I'll actually tackle him to the ground or not. That would probably draw undue attention. I might just let him go.

"I have to go to the bathroom," says Blake.

"Hold it."

"Is that *truly* the risk you want to take? Do I look like somebody with flawless bladder control?"

"I have to go too. We'll go together."

"Oh, yay."

I get out of the car, keeping a close eye on Blake's seat belt and the possibility that it might pop loose at any moment.

By the way, if you're one of those people who buys a book and then skips around in it, it's possible that this is the first page you're reading. Let me assure you that I'm *not* the bad guy. Blake is horrible. I'm not going to go so far as to say that my behavior is justified, but at least skim the first twenty-five chapters, okay? Then you'll understand.

I swipe my debit card.

The electronic display on the gas pump informs me that the transaction has been declined.

I swipe it again.

Declined.

I almost swipe it a third time but decide I can't handle that much rejection. Was it insufficient funds? I thought I had enough money in my bank account to get me to California, but I also have to concede that planning is not my strongest personality trait right now.

"Do you have a credit card?" I ask Blake.

"For what?"

"Gas."

"You didn't bring gas money?"

"It won't take my card."

Blake stares at me for a while. "You're a very poor kidnapper."

"I know."

"Am I gonna get reimbursed?"

"How about we split the costs? You owe me that at least."

Blake rolls down the window and hands me a credit card.

"Thank you."

"You realize they can trace it, right?"

"Yeah. If I'm worried about a credit card transaction being traced, I'll know it's gone too far."

"Fair enough."

I fill up the tank and give Blake back his credit card. I can't deny that I'm quite a bit less devoted to the idea of driving him all the way to California now. It sounded okay while in the midst of a nervous breakdown, but I feel like there will be a lot of reasons to say, "Oops."

We go into the gas station, and I generously allow him to use the restroom. I suppose he could leave a message for the next person, but as with the credit card tracing, if I hit the point where I'm doing a sweep of a restroom to make sure that Blake hasn't left any messages, our road trip has gone too far.

We get back in my car, and I still haven't decided if I'm going to turn around and head for home or if I'm going to pretend that the California trip is still on.

What would you do? Be honest.

Not kidnap Blake in the first place? Thanks. That's real helpful. I bet you would've given a real answer if Katniss Everdeen asked for advice.

I decide to continue toward California. Let Blake sweat

it out for a while longer and hope that he'll learn his lesson. If I'm lucky, he'll start sobbing and pleading for mercy and promising to help me put my life back to normal before it's time to fill up the tank again.

And then my car breaks down.

27.

I'M ABLE TO get my sputtering car off to the side of the road before it stops working. Black smoke billows from underneath the front hood.

"Do you think it's going to explode?" Blake asks.

"No, but we should get out."

We hurriedly exit the vehicle and move far enough away that we won't be struck by flaming debris if it blows up.

"I take back all the things I've said about your car," says Blake. "It's a fine, reliable automobile." He coughs, even though we're not in range of the smoke anymore. "I'd call a tow truck, but some very intelligent person threw away my phone."

I pull out my own phone. This would be a wonderfully ironic moment to discover that my battery is dead, but I've still got seventy-one percent left, so it's cool.

"You're bad at everything, aren't you?" asks Blake.

I punch him in the face.

Unlike my previous laughable efforts, this is a pretty darn good punch. It gets him right in the jaw. He lets out a grunt of pain, and his knees wobble.

Having done this, I suddenly suffer the emotional anguish of knowing that I've resorted to violence as well as the physical pain of how much the punch hurt my hand.

Blake looks like he's going to topple over, but he doesn't. Should I give him a gentle shove?

He looks really mad. Scary mad. Like if this were a very different type of book, I'd expect his skin to split open and reveal the demonic creature inside.

I almost feel like I should offer him one free punch to even things out.

He leaps at me. I throw another punch. I was not on the receiving end of this punch and thus cannot say this from personal experience, but I'm pretty sure that getting punched in the face hurts a lot more when you were in the middle of leaping at somebody.

He stumbles backward, trips, and falls to the ground.

Then he gets back up, growls (I always assumed that I'd have a good laugh if somebody actually growled at me, but nope.), and charges at me.

I don't know any fancy martial arts moves, so I settle for letting him tackle me. We both crash to the ground.

I'm surprised that nobody has pulled over to offer us a ride, but it could have something to do with the fact that we're currently beating each other up.

He punches me in the face. It hurts worse than my hand did when I punched him in the face.

I try to punch him in the face, but my fist brushes across his earlobe. If he wore an earring, it might have caught on my hand, doing major damage, but he doesn't, so this punch has little effect on the outcome of our fight.

He punches me in the index finger, probably by accident. He doesn't break it or anything. But my finger bends backward a bit more than it's supposed to, and it does not feel good at all. I cry out in pain.

Though multiple parts of my body hurt, at least I'm not embarrassing myself the way I did last time we wrestled. It's important to always improve.

We punch each other in the face at the exact same time.

Our faces hurt. Our hands hurt. And I feel like we're both wishing this fight was over. I'm in the mood to cry some more.

"Why did you do it?" I wail.

"Do what?"

"Ruin my life!"

"I don't know what you're talking about!" he cries.

"Yes, you do! Why did you do it? That's all I want to know! Is it because you're jealous of me?"

"No!"

"Are you sure?"

"How could I be jealous of you? You're poor!"

"I had a girlfriend and a band!"

"I have a girlfriend!"

"No, you don't!"

"She lives in Canada!"

"You are lying! You don't text or call anyone from home!"

"She visits on weekends!"

I punch the ground. Obviously, I meant to punch Blake instead. But the ground is softer than his body, and it's actually a nice change of pace.

"Why did you do it?" I demand.

"I didn't!"

"Is it because you're evil?"

"I don't believe in the concept of evil!"

"A different question then! How much did it cost to bribe everybody to attend our show at the Lane?"

"I didn't bribe them!"

"Yes, you did!"

I punch the ground again. This time it is on purpose.

"Ten bucks," Blake admits.

"Each?"

"Yes."

"Okay. Ten bucks isn't that big of a bribe."

"It was like five hundred bucks to get all those people to go."

"Right, but the individual bribes weren't that big. For ten bucks, they'd still have to kind of want to see the show, right?"

"I guess."

"It was an incentive, but it can't have been the whole reason they went."

"How much did you *think* I spent?"

"I don't know. Fifty bucks?"

"That would've been twenty-five hundred dollars."

"If I can imagine you spending one thousand dollars to bribe people, I can imagine twenty-five hundred. How rich are you anyway?"

"I shouldn't have spent that money. My mom is gonna kill me."

"Can we stop fighting now?" I ask.

Blake punches me in the arm.

"You can't punch me after I call for a truce!"

"I didn't accept the truce. That was a fair punch."

"Please tell me it cost more than ten bucks each to turn the kids in school against me."

Blake nods. "My mom is going to be furious."

"Then why did you do it!"

"I don't know!"

"Yes, you do! You have to know!"

"I don't!"

"Were you going to start dressing like me and take over my life?"

"No!"

"Are you sure? You weren't trying to date Audrey and be the lead singer of Fanged Grapefruit?"

"I can't sing!"

"I know that, but maybe you don't!"

"I wasn't trying to assume your identity!"

"Were you doing research for a novel?"

"No!"

"Are you sure?"

"Quit asking if I'm sure! I think I'd know if I was doing research for a novel or not! I don't like to read!"

"That doesn't mean you don't want to inflict your torture on people who like to read! This was research! Admit it!"

"Are you saying that I'm trying to ruin your life to research a book about another kid who's trying to ruin his cousin's life?" Blake asks, bewildered.

"Well, it wouldn't necessarily have to be his cousin," I admit.

"Listen to yourself, Rod."

"I am! I've been listening to myself this whole time! But I'm out of ideas! I need to know why you did this! Was it a bet?" I prompt.

Blake doesn't say anything.

"A bet?" I ask. "This was a bet?"

Blake shrugs.

"You ruined my life for a bet? You wiener!"

"Are you going to hit me again if I say yes?"

"I'll stop hitting you if you tell the truth."

"Okay."

"Will you stop hitting me if I stop hitting you for telling the truth?" I ask.

"Yes," says Blake.

"Deal. Was this really a bet?"

"Yes."

"With who?"

"Myself."

"What?" Even for Blake that makes no sense.

"I made a bet with myself."

I want to hit him again, but that would be a violation of the terms of our agreement. "What do you mean you made a bet with yourself?"

"I was jealous, okay? When my parents told me I'd be

staying with you, I was really mad about uprooting my life for them to take a trip without me. And I expected you to have a miserable life. And when you weren't miserable, it made me feel bad about my own life and how miserable I felt being away from home. So I figured I could salvage the situation by making you feel worse so that I'd feel better."

A car pulls off to the side of the road next to us. An old man in a cowboy hat gets out.

"Are you two fellows okay?" he asks.

"Yeah, we're good," I assure him.

"Not really a safe place to be arguin'."

"We know. We know," I say. "We've stopped. We were just about to get up."

"Want me to call you a tow truck? Your car is lookin' a little combustible."

"Nah, we're fine. We were going to finish up our discussion, and then I was going to call somebody. Thanks for stopping to help though. We appreciate it."

The man tips his hat to us. "You two have a good day then. Make sure you put some ice on those bruises. They're pretty ghastly." He gets back in his car and drives off.

Blake and I stand up.

"Okay, so you were saying?" I ask.

"Right. I figured you'd be wallowing in self-pity. That's what I'd be doing in your place. But then I discovered that you were happy. Genuinely happy. You had a girlfriend. Not as hot as mine, but still. And even though your band was clearly awful—"

"We're not awful."

"Yeah, you are."

"I'm going to disagree with that."

"Maybe it's your genre. Nobody actually likes punk rock music. They might say they do, but they're faking it."

"Don't make me break our truce."

"Anyway, what I saw is that you were playing music in front of people and loving it. I couldn't believe it. You were happy. You had this sad excuse for a life and absolutely no reason to enjoy it, and yet you were happy."

"Yeah, I was," I say, thinking wistfully back to my life before Blake arrived.

"And so I bet myself that I could ruin it for you."

If I'm not going to hit him, I feel like the only proper reaction to this is to stare at him, slack-jawed, for about three hours.

Instead I ask, "What were the stakes?"

"No ice cream for a year."

"Seriously?"

"Starting when I got back home, of course. I'd need ice cream to make it through those three months at your place."

"What did you get if you won?"

"Nothing," says Blake. "I wouldn't reward myself for ruining somebody's life. That would be wrong."

I punch him.

Yes, it's a low move to punch somebody in the middle of a truce, but there were extenuating circumstances. Dude ruined my life, and he didn't even do it for extra ice cream.

It's the best punch of the fight so far. Perfect placement to the jaw, superb follow-through with my fist, and it doesn't even hurt my hand all that much, although that could be the result of my sheer blinding rage.

As the guy in the cowboy hat pointed out, the side of the highway is not an ideal place to be fighting. Much can go wrong. Let's look at the following example, in which a sixteen-year-old kid punches his cousin in the face. The cousin, rather than falling to the ground in a heap, stumbles backward in a daze.

Under normal circumstances, the act of stumbling backward in a daze immediately after receiving a punch to the face is not such a big deal. Sure, the subject could trip and injure his or her tailbone or accidentally bump into a table and knock over somebody's cup of coffee, but it's not typically life-threatening.

The problem with the stumbling occurring in this particular location is that there's a road right there. And this isn't some tiny dirt road where horse-drawn carriages are on their way to purchase supplies for the long winter. This is a road with lots of fast cars.

So when I punched Blake and he stumbled, a car was headed right for him. I won't deny that I felt a strong sense of regret about throwing that particular punch, which will stay with me for the rest of my ruined life.

28.

NO, I DON'T just stand there and let Blake get run over by a car! I don't even *consider* doing that! Jeez! What kind of person do you think I am?

It's not like a semi is barreling down upon him. It is, in fact, a very tiny, economically priced, two-door sedan that I'm sure gets excellent gas mileage. Still, it's going seventy miles per hour, and there's little question that it will splatter Blake on impact.

There's no time to grab him by the arm and pull him back to safety. If I miss his arm, he's doomed. My only choice is to dive at him and knock him out of the way. I might die. If I do, I apologize for the abrupt ending of—

29.

SORRY. DIDN'T MEAN to end that last chapter so soon. I was distracted by the car.

I dive at Blake and push him out of harm's way. We both fall onto the shoulder of the road.

The driver of the tiny car blares his horn as he zips past us.

I stand and help Blake to his feet.

His eyes are wide. "You…you saved my life."

"You would have done the same thing," I say.

Blake shakes his head. "Nope."

Another horn honks. I glance to my right in time to see a semitruck barreling down the highway.

Blake dives at me, pushing us out of harm's way. We both tumble onto the grass by the side of the highway.

"Okay, maybe I would have," says Blake. "That's surprising."

We both lie there for a minute, catching our breath and trying to recover from the shock.

"You saved my life," says Blake. "You endangered it, and then you saved it. How can we be enemies when we're willing to sacrifice ourselves for each other?"

"I don't know," I admit. "It seems stupid."

"This is a bond we can't break. We'll always have this moment."

"I'm sorry I kidnapped you," I say.

"I'm sorry I ruined your life."

"I appreciate your apology."

"What if I try to repair the damage I've done?"

"That would be cool."

"I've been a terrible cousin. But I think we should start from scratch. I understand why you were happy. And I'd like to be happy like that too."

"Really?"

Could this be the start of an actual friendship? I'm going to say no, probably not, but maybe it's the beginning of an era when Blake and I can cohabitate. I'm certainly willing to try to make things better.

We get to our feet again.

"Your car's on fire," says Blake.

"I see that." I sigh. "You know, it really was a terrible car."

"It was all right. It got us this far."

"Are you trying to write song lyrics?" I ask with a smile.

"What?"

"Song lyrics."

"Huh?"

"What you said rhymed with what I said. *Car* and *far* rhyme."

"Oh. No, I wasn't trying to write song lyrics."

"I didn't actually think you were. I was making a joke."

"Hmm."

I give him a playful punch on the shoulder. He gives me a playful punch back. I think the punches hurt both of us, but we don't want to say anything.

It may sound weird, but I truly believe that Blake and I are going to be fine from now on. Am I glad he came into my life? Not particularly. Have we gained a new respect for each other? I dunno. Maybe if you really stretch the definition of respect. But when we were about to get splattered on the highway, we both risked our lives for each other, and that means something.

The next two and a half months aren't going to be so bad.

I take out my cell phone. I missed a call from Mom while we were fighting, so I call her back.

"Where are you?" she asks.

"Um, on our way to Mel's. What's up?"

"Aunt Mary and Uncle Clark canceled their cruise.

Everybody on the ship got food poisoning. Blake needs to come home and pack his stuff because they booked him a flight home tonight."

Yes, I truly believe that Blake and I would have gotten along for the next several weeks, but let's be honest. This is better.

30.

HEY, IT'S ALMOST over! I want to thank you for sharing this experience with me. I'd like to apologize again for that part where I got mad at you and switched to another book. It was inappropriate, and I'm glad you stuck with me even when I wasn't being a good host. I'll make it up to you if there's a sequel.

It's a few weeks later. There are no more rodent posters on my walls. Nobody keeps me up at night with their snoring. Things are pretty much back to normal, except that this guy let a whole bunch of potbellied pigs loose in our neighborhood. It was crazy! I want to tell you all about it, but it would be weird to resolve the story of my cousin Blake by launching into an unrelated story about a pig rampage. If you ever come to one of my shows, ask me, and I'll tell you the whole story.

Did Audrey and I get back together? Wouldn't that be a good ending? Except we didn't. Blake offered to send her an email with a full account of his cruel deeds, but we decided that it might be better if we kept each other's problematic behavior (like, y'know, a case of light kidnapping) a secret. I trust you won't say anything either.

Anyway, Audrey already pretty much knew what Blake had done when she broke up with me, but I'm working to earn back her trust and respect. Blake didn't bring out the best in me, but we're back to being good lab partners. She doesn't have a new boyfriend yet, and I don't have a new girlfriend, so you never know…

Did Fanged Grapefruit get back together? No. Wait, yes! After Blake flew home and I was putting my own posters back on the wall, I felt really bad about how I botched the performances. So the next day at school, I told Mel and Clarissa that they could keep the Fanged Grapefruit name and use any of the songs that they wanted.

Mel and Clarissa said that they felt awful about what happened, so I could keep the name and the songs.

I said no, it was all my fault, and they deserved the name and songs.

They said that they should have been more understanding about all I was going through and that they couldn't in good conscience keep the name and the songs.

I said it was a shame to waste them.

They said, "Perhaps we could both use them."

I said, "Do you mean we should get the band back together?"

They said, "Maybe."

So yes, Fanged Grapefruit continues to play every Monday night at the Lane. We've changed things up a bit. Mel is now the lead singer, and I'm now lead guitar, which is how it should have been in the first place. But I still get to ask the audience if they're ready to rock.

And guess what? A few of the people who were paid to be there came to see us again!

Mom did want to know how my car had caught on fire three hours from home and also why Blake and I looked like we'd been beating each other up when we got home. We basically said that we'd gone to scope out new places for gigs. We couldn't come up with a good way to explain our injuries, so we admitted that we'd gotten into a fight because of the stress we felt when my car broke down.

Did she believe us? Yes. Am I grounded? Oh yeah. Excluding my Monday night performances, I'm pretty much grounded until summer. And obviously, I don't have a car anymore. So I don't want to give the impression that this is a *completely* happy ending.

That said, things could've worked out worse. They could be scraping me off the tires of that semi. And the videos of me messing up my performance could've gone viral. (I assume they will when Fanged Grapefruit hits it big, but by then I'll be able to laugh about it.)

Will Blake and I stay in touch? Since we're almost done here and I don't want to end on a bitter note, I'm going to go ahead and say sure. In fact, I'll text him right now.

Hey.

Hey.

What's up?

Not much. How's your book going?

Good. Almost done.

Do I come off badly in it?

No, not at all.

Are you still going with present tense, even though it will confuse readers who want to know if you're running back and forth to your computer to type things up as they happen?

I think my readers will grant me creative license.

Well, I've got to go pick my Canadian girlfriend up at the airport. She should be through customs now.

See ya, Blake.

See ya.

So yeah, even though having my cousin move in with me for a few weeks wasn't the best experience of my life, it turns out that I like writing, and it was good material for a book. So here we are. This has been Rod Conklin, lead guitar of Fanged Grapefruit. Get home safely, and I hope you enjoyed the show!

ENCORE!

Dedicated to my cousin Blake.

Got a cousin named Blake. (Blake! Blake!)
Yeah, a cousin named Blake. (Blake! Blake!)
Oh, I can't stand Blake.
Wanna throw him in a lake.
Abandon him during an earthquake.
Or deny him a slice of cake.
He keeps me awake.
And he's such a snake.
His face I'd like to break.
Hope he gets a toothache.
Wish I didn't have a cousin named Blake. (Blake! Blake!)
My life would be greatly improved without the existence of
*   my cousin named Blake. (Blake! Blake!)*
He's a great big ol' fake.
Trust him? A mistake.

Think it's time to make.

A pointy wooden stake.

Hope he steps on a rake.

And spills his milkshake.

And gets an overcooked steak.

He's one I'd like to forsake.

*I'd spend every day walking around with a big grin on my
face and whistling merry tunes if not for my cousin
named Blake. (Blake! Blake!)*

*Yeah, I'd be insufferable about my love for the world around
me and my appreciation for all of the beauty in nature,
but it's all messed up because of my cousin named Blake.
(Blake! Blake!)*

I don't like you, Blake.

Really don't like you, Blake.

You're quite unlikable, Blake.

I'm just no fan of Blake.

There are still other words that rhyme with Blake.

Like bake and Jake and slake and flake.

And spake and partake and remake and opaque.

But I think I'm done rhyming with Blake.

Ladies and gentlemen, good night!

The End

ACKNOWLEDGMENTS

It takes more than one person to ruin somebody's life. Thanks to Elizabeth Boyer, Justin Dimos, Donna Fitzpatrick, Lynne Hansen, Sarah Kasman, Kathryn Lynch, Michael McBride, Jim Morey, Annette Pollert-Morgan, Rhonda Rettig, Stefani Sloma, Paul Synuria II, and Alex Yeadon for their efforts in making this book not suck.

ABOUT THE AUTHOR

Jeff Strand's ridiculous novels include *A Bad Day for Voodoo*, *I Have a Bad Feeling about This*, *The Greatest Zombie Movie Ever*, *Stranger Things Have Happened*, and a bunch of others. After over twenty years in Florida, he now lives in Atlanta, Georgia. You can follow him on Twitter @jeffstrand and visit his website at jeffstrand.com.